I0708325

MOIETIES
by
Elytron Frass

MOIETIES

A Subtle Body Press Book

Alex Oleszewski | CEO
Cliff Hensley | Managing Director, Editor-in-Chief
Cori Hart | Creative Director, Senior Designer

FIRST EDITION, May 28, 2024

Co-Edited by [x]
Design and Layout by Elytron Frass
Typeset in 1651 Alchemy and Instant Karma

ISBN 979-8-9854370-3-4

Library of Congress Cataloging-in-Publication Data available upon request.

Subtle Body Press, LLC
7901 4th St N STE 8671, St. Petersburg, FL, 33702
www.subtlebodypress.com

PRAISE & ACKNOWLEDGEMENTS

How far shall we go to be reunited, even if it should destroy us? This is the question at the heart of Elytron Frass's Moieties, a meditation on the mystical dictum that pure being, the immediate oneness of Pleroma, is for us indistinguishable from absolute nothing. In pursuit of this revelation, Moieties pushes past the formal and material limits of the novel itself, which must be read forwards, backwards, and out of sequence if the inquisitive reader is to extract its truth. This work transpires in a mise en abyme, in two parts which mirror one another and converge on a central point that can only be inferred from its reflections. Though we glimpse it askew, the halves fuse in a Gnostic syzygy, in which the separations of inner and outer, one and other, love and death, come crashing together into oblivion.

G R E G O R Y * M A R K S

An ero guro dark fantasia set in a sprawling gnostic open-world, Elytron Frass's Moieties is a complex artefact. A cornucopia of rich imagery, archetypes, and design, it thematizes symmetry and simultaneity through an intricate interweaving of form and content. Five concurrent narratives blossom across the pages together, like a necrotic fairytale garden whose evil flowers meet and melt and meld together, in an orgiastic rite of spring. With shamanic abandon, Frass demonstrates that, in the digital era, novels need not revel in their obsolescence; instead, they can molt into something multiplicitous, bold, and new. Moieties is a relentless, visionary work that doesn't ask for a skim; it demands your attention. And, once it has you gripped, it won't be read; it will be activated.

L O G A N * B E R R Y

For Glossa Lac, who bleeds an out to which I drown in

Perhaps there was always a cleft in my brain through which you could register. A part of your voice which would grow louder and louder the further and further you'd distance yourself from my wanting proximity. The loathsome years spent questioning how, when, and where, or if, you'd reveal yourself—only receiving half-answers, half-truths, half-hearted reassurances until that unrequited and semicircling ouroboros of desire for our rapture, my serpentine finger, hooked on that wriggling, shrinking, recoiling length of your phantom tongue, worming itself deeper inside of my skull.

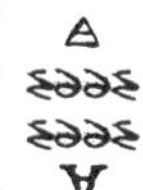

Whenever I would advance, you'd retreat because we were other and ever asynchronous—two incompatible, opposite unequivocals. I'd later find myself clinging with lust to a figment of you that your voice insisted existed in some alternate Gnostic reality that would only be brought into this one through some sort of tragic reunion with me—and so I searched far and wide in the garden of lack I'd been scouring in for that exact ladder or shoot which would lead me to you while becoming eclipsed by a roiling hatred stained tarry black—an obsidian mirror, where all sorts of fantasies were projected, wherein your long overdue revelation to me begged for defilement and erasure by my fervent hands.

Subject L is being prepared for a novel separation surgery from Subject R, her conjoined brother.

SS   SS   SS

Dumped with other shunned bodies from one of the apertures fixed in the clouds and into a wheezing, reviving volcano, I'd been deemed dead on arrival by the discerning Eyes of Pleroma. In their judicial yet dolorous way, they'd gaze ever down on creation through the very apertures which had expelled us. I was expected to seek and unite with each of the Seven Enigmas. There were six neighboring islands circumscribing the one that I occupied, and each contained at least one of seven Enigmas. The islands' names were Pergamum, Smyrna, Sardis, Laodicea, Thyatira, and Ephesus.

The garbage heap island of Pargamum was a landfill of floating debris and it was ruled by the one called the Salvager. The zoological island of Smyrna was overrun by ravenous beasts and overseen by the one called the Animal. The hyper-industrialized island of Sardis was an utterly automated, fully mechanical structure, ruled by the one called the Mainframe. The libidinal island of Laodicea was wholly an organ of flesh and was ruled by the one called the Fetishist. The glass island of Thyatira was a cemetery of mirrors, which entombed all the darkness it could, and was ruled by the one called the Lucent. The sunken island of Ephesus, where stood the Museum of Alchemical Marriage, was overseen by the one called the Lover.

They are craniopagus sesquizygotic Siamese twins of opposite sex—an anomaly layered in implausibility, accentuated by oddity. Thus, with Subject L born female, and Subject R, male, they are semi-identical yet fused together at a portion of the skull.

HOLY HALL TRI SPI SINK INTO AMOR CHASMS CHA MOR NAT INTO HUM DUST

I was cajoled into thinking that I contained but a symbolon of a human being—that is to say I'd been born with just half of a sternum, absent from midline to right, meant to be fused with half of another's. Yet the search for that other would lead me astray and leave me lastingly stranded. I was hunting and hungering like the ill-fated fiend, fallen into addiction's abyss—seeker of an impossible sustenance inseparable from starvation. Within you, you said, dwells a moiety of the divine that can be liberated from the material world should you acquire the key and the knowledge needed to use it. But I couldn't see the trap for what it was through the fog of your influence. The only thing visible was the dangling fruit of your promise—that of returning to God without the burden of existential duration, without the terrors that come with beginnings or ends.

Paradoxically, it was Yahweh's rejection of me, not my secret desire for Godhead, which had been accepted with pride—for I was less volatile as something deformed, halved, and more wholesome despite it. That you'd convince me to find a new calling: to find completion by way of the flesh (or more specifically, by the sternum) proved cruel and deserving of loathing. Uniting myself to my divine opposite promised the key to get out of the world and return to the firmament where I belonged. I hadn't yet grown

---

Subjects L and R are the first of their kind. However, Subject L's brother is prone to frequent atonic seizures which greatly debilitate the quality of life for both siblings.

weary of the worldly cycles—laudably sentient atrocities instigated at birth, that find brief respite following our deaths. I wanted for their ebb and flow to situate under my thumb at my whim instead of Yahweh's. I aspired for dominion. I was a perfectly mutable being; I would transform myself to oppose and vanquish each one of the Seven Enigmas. All this I believed because you, that partly audible voice in my head, had convinced me. And, so, I anointed myself as I'd been instructed to do in a puddle of the tears that now and again would rain down from the dolorous Eyes of Pleroma, and having neither clothes nor weapons, crafted the tools that I'd need from within me.

With your galvanic but incomplete guidance, I moved on all fours as if feral, skin blemished with ash, over tremulous volcanic soot, and surprisingly warm human bodies—whose faces pressed into the quavering ground—most, if not all, appearing to be male and of similar pallor and stature to mine. I was concerned with maintaining my footing upon such convulsive terrain. I trudged through the bodies without much regard as to whether they were dead or alive until I had reached the volcanic mouth's lowest depression. It was there that the bodies within this vast mass showed signs of harrowing injury—their necks crushed, broken, constricted, or twisted by rope, wire or chainlink—impossible for them to have survived. Ones with their faces turned skyward revealed to be bluish clones

---

The twins currenlty live with their mother and father, who oversee their home education.

of myself expressing pure and unspeakable ecstasy. Their identical hands stroked identical cocks, uninterrupted by my intrusion. In the center of this lewd congregation, I'd find the first of the Seven Enigmas. The one known as the Garroter resided on this very island (the only island which you'd never name) and was the builder of densely packed gallows of torture stocks, garrotes, gibbets, and breaking wheels. Each of these treacherous devices were occupied by one or more of my duplicates—who, though ensnared, ceaselessly drooled from their phalli and, moreover, hung there undying, defiantly blissful. In the middle of all of those creaking devices, the Garroter—an obese dark-skinned woman draped in a wide cyan naqaab and abaya—knelt down beside some passive likeness of me. With bare hands trembling she'd been strangling him to no avail as he gurgled and wheezed with delight—his erection a fleshy, pulsing arc of vile and mocking euphoria. Tears started to flow from her bitter, defeated, dolorous eyes. The Eyes of Pleroma observed her futile attempts, before letting go of their lacrimal own. There began a steady rain. Both she and the Eyes wouldn't let up. Stepping over libidinous, deathless clones, I approached —she and I both drenched and shivering.

More of my likenesses fell from the heavens— a new batch of living cadavers to be piled atop of the old. I kept light on my feet,

---

Their parents consent to their participation. The subjects have six months remaining before they are no longer minors.

dodging a fast-falling body that nearly col-
lided with me. This brought me back to the
Plague Years, when I was a child—not the
action of dodging so much as the abundance
of heaps of limp bodies—the charnel grounds,
which we'd turned into our playgrounds,
where my sister and I had grown up in in-
decent times on the plains of the Mainland.

Having raised ourselves we relied only
on instincts we half understood and incomplete faiths which we were still piec-
ing together, to validate our otherwise
meaningless place in that frigid plot of
the world. Mandrakes would jut from
the navels and nostrils of all of the dead. We'd
pick and we'd pluck then we'd hop, skip, and
jump from one belly-up thing to the next—
making trampolines of postmortem disten-
tion, pouncing down hard so they'd release
pressurized blowouts of florid corpse fauna
and flora. We'd see all of which the gangrenous deceased had been brewing inside.

I interrupted the Garroter's attempted murder with a gesture both playful and menac-
ing. Care to try your hand at me? I asked,
knowing that she would and what to do
once she did because you'd whispered it
to me. Perhaps this was the first time in a
long while that anyone, my other selves included, had addressed her; she quickly recoiled in shock and astonishment. I stood
over her then, a soaked shroud of dark hair

SOME WILL FUCK MUR
THEY LOVE TO BECOME
BREACH ABOVES FR
FORM IS ONLY HALF

AN FRACTION OF THEE
BIND THEE CHAINS TO

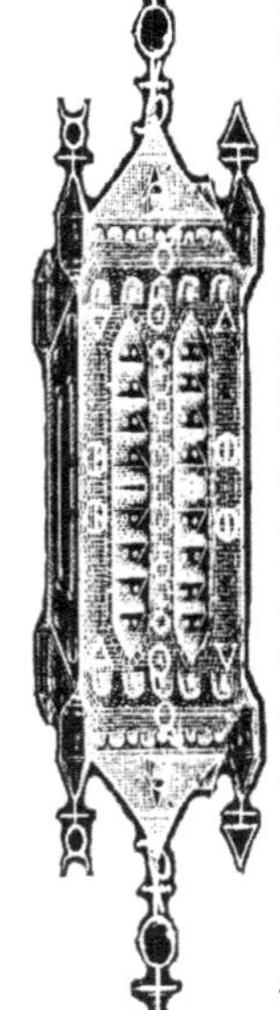

---

*Upon social history intake Subjects L and R appear ap-
prehensive. The twins inquire if they will be punished
for having committed unspecified sins.*

in my eyes. I knelt across from her to meet directly at those cyan-tinged irises. It was only her eyes and the bridge of her nose that were showing—her wide cyan naqaab and abaya concealing everything else. Without unlocking my stare, I took her swollen and quivering hands in my own. I placed hers on my throat and released all my breath in her face. Although I was surrendering to the Garroter, I needed it to be known that she should still consider me her nemesis.

You coward! You're just like all the rest, she rasped through her pale bluish garments. You won't transcend. At the last moment you'll fear for your coming death and deny it from passing—living on instead as though something dead yet undying due to the horror the thought of death brings—incessantly masturbating within your inertia of fear.

I didn't dare to reply out of respect for my enemy. As the Garroter worked herself up, chastising me, her stranglehold firmed and gradually tightened. I dared not close my eyes once I felt my airway begin to occlude. There came the threat of an instance of pleasure—a desire for pain and arousal—which, with force, I averted right out of my mind. I kept my arms slack at my sides and forbade my phallus from rising. My eyes bulged and my heart molded into a rock-solid fist, punching out from inside of my chest. Having overcome asphyxiation's erogenous impulse, my

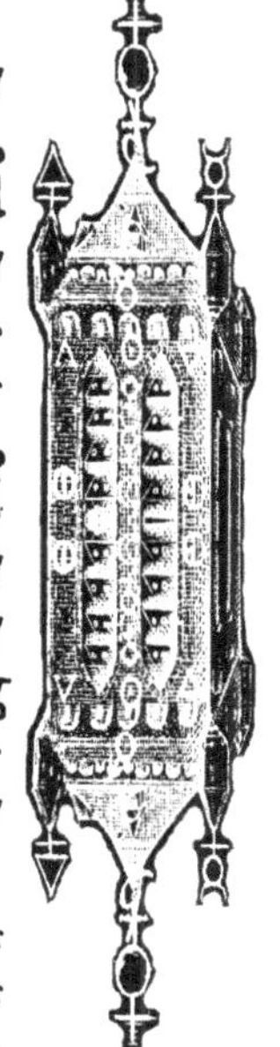

All parties are assured that the administrators of this experimental procedure are not affiliated with a religious organization.

whole being flushed cyanotic with panic and begged me to gasp for a fresh breath of air.

And she, the Garroter, taunted me thus: I know you too well by now. At the very last second, you'll beg for oxygen, and you'll breathe it in like all other weaklings. You will loosen my grip from your throat with one hand, and you'll rub yourself off with the other. Your body will live, and your spirit will suffocate in its torpidity. Just look around you! Weep for your previous failures. You won't oppose me. I will win, as I always have won.

I remained defiantly passive and even encouraged her to keep choking me out because of that defiance. I had become the Victim Divine. I played at her game to prevail, and soon she would learn that I'd come here to die by her hands as a means to defeat her. My heart was slowing, and blood was turning to thick bluish sludge in my veins—my lungs and esophagus, indescribably aching, consciousness slipping away. And I welcomed it. Life left as I had required it to. I felt my spine shatter apart, brittle column of glass. My throat was crushed thin by her palms.

The volcano awoke. There was nothing that she could have done to reverse it. The ground shook beneath my cowardly duplicates, lying in asphyxia's stupor. The ashen earth between bodies fractured, hissing open and seething. Smoke and a wrath full of heat

---

The subjects and their parents are recent apostates from an undisclosed ecclesiastical denomination.

rose from the vents. Magma was spewing—my likenesses burst into flame. My soul split from that place before the volcano erupted, yet the Garroter's hadn't. Her eyes bulged like my own as she realized how I had entrapped her. There was no time for her to escape, so she strained to endure and squeeze tighter and tighter around me. We remained like that, kneeling next to each other, her hold on me merely corporeal, until both of us were incinerated by the volcanic explosion.

Ever a heavenly reject, I was once again dumped like hot trash from an aperture in the sky. Yet the island and body which I inhabited this time were different. I'd been curled up on my side on the scabrous edge of Laodicea, dressed in full-body obsidian latex—with a gasmask rebreather sealing in tension between itself and my head; there were outgoing tubes at the left ear and the mouth which slackly extended beyond the horizon line of that flesh covered island. Laodicea closely resembled the dorsal view of a brain with a large central eye. A thick, low-lying fog clung about it. The ground before me was soft and mucosal, covered in masses of lesser eyes—some as small as my head, others much more cyclopean but all very dolorous and overwhelmingly pitiful. Those sad gazes locked onto mine and followed wherever I'd go. I made sure to avoid contact with them after one had exploded on me at the touch of my naked finger. Its gore was projectile and

----

The twins' mother and father claim that their faith had been steeped in 'scarring, insidious, and manipulative' dualist mythology.

of a yellowish bile. That naked finger in question—which had been exposed due to a slit in the glove of my latex—was instantly blighted with boils and blisters which blossomed with miniscule messes of desolate, angelic eyes.

Widening the cut in my outfit, I set my left hand entirely free. I laid my palm on the landmass—its leery eyes, a garden of televisions, signaling in scrambled alien pornography. Our libidinal gazes tempted towards mutual ruin. In rapid response Laodicea's adipose tissues budded with marks of disease, corruption, and wear—all localized to wherever I'd touch it. Between weeping lesions and darkening bruises, those angelic Eyes of Pleroma projected deep agony and despair. My hand also flowered adversely in symptoms of touch: an acute, white-hot burning. My palm, like my finger before it, blistered with masses of various sizes of eyes.

To either my fortune or lack thereof, I could not see from their pupils. I shrugged off the sting of the malady, touching again my palm's largest blistering eye to one which was plaguing Laodicea. The two exploded on impact, agonizingly synchronized. A red void had gored into my palm; a blood-pooling socket replaced Laodicea's parasite eye. You'd butt in to critique its ocular outburst, and mine, as sensual mutualism repressed, but I drowned out your captious niggling with blood and desirous thoughts of arterial labyrinths,

Subjects L and R collectively identify themselves as 'I' and 'we' interchangeably but consistently do so in vocal unison.

socket-to-socket—the colliding and mixing of oppositional redflow, breathing only in shades known to heme, washing my lungs in those crimson perceptions, the prelude to finer outlets of violence which I lusted after.

The porous blobs of fat framing each of Laodicea's eyes made up most of the glistening terrain and conformed to the shape of my latex soles and one-gloved hand as I scrambled over its mound-face—hoisting myself up on odd shafts of lash-like projections, whenever available. Looking back into the waters surrounding the island, I could see— jutting from certain shoreline locations—the island's long-curled, platinum hair flowing, limp talons sprawling between semi-submerged, colossal, extensive, gray-feathered avian wings. I wondered if the island's whole coast sprouted with these in this fashion. The hair moved like kelp from a seabed, and the manner in which the waves washed over the talons and wings made them appear too resigned, or too weakened, too injured or paralyzed to ever latch on or take flight again.

I was provided with no further insight while traversing Laodicea. You'd gone silent and still. My mind had returned to folding upon its own desolation. I'd given up trying to rouse your attention. You made it quite clear that you only cared to speak at me, not

---

The twins present with a mild cognitive delay; they are slow to reply or react when questioned or introduced to new stimuli but have otherwise normal retention and recall of memory. When they do reply or react to physical stimuli, their motor skills are expressed with a seemingly effortless synchronicity.

with me, whenever you'd something to say. I wanted either much more or nothing from you, but what you were willing to give was barely a resonant earful. When you did attempt to say something, there upon Laodicea, the feminine voice of another—distinct for its crisp and overtly sensual tone—interjected and spoke over yours through the tube in my mask, situated at my left ear hole.

Where have you gone? Why have you strayed? Don't you recall what transpired last time? Have you succumbed to amnesia? Tread carefully, please, cautioned the sensual voice, the exquisite creature which hosts us is of the same caste of angels that gaze down from those apertures in the clouds. This one somehow, some time ago, fell from above to the sea. An erogenous object—it isn't some sexless abstraction of ether but instead a beguiling, wanton carnality, haplessly loosened from God. And yet, as we already know, unprotected physical contact with it would despoil us both. What restrained pleasures we've reaped through our rubber clad covenants have sufficed well enough to sustain us while stranded together out here on its beach.

She thought she was speaking to whomever's body I now possessed. I could only presume that this was the voice of the Fetishist. Not yet prepared to reply to her inquiries,

---

Upon further examination, cone beam computed tomography scans reveal that the subjects' brains are connected from Subject L's right hemisphere to Subject R's left hemisphere by an additional corpus callosum, which bridges the large fenestration between their fused skulls.

I followed the two immeasurable lengths of those latex tubes coming out from my mask. The fog thickened as I progressed. Rendered nigh blind in those palpable mists, I relied on the tubes as a guide to the top of the largest and most central eye of Laodicea. It was like climbing a rather steep hill. The trek up was steady but slow, until my tubes became suddenly taut like a leash; I was briskly reeled upwards and onto its summit. The tubes of my mask were being sucked into the black of its pupil. Once standing over its glazed and woeful convexity, I was gently pulled onto my knees then closer still until I'd been laid face-down atop it. On the other side of its lens, within the obsidian moat of the eye, the faint latex silhouette of the Fetishist faced me. She was weightlessly floating within it. The tubes coming out at the mouth and right ear regions of her latex mask were connected to those at my left ear hole and mouth, respectively; moreover, there was no slack on our tubes; they'd apparently shortened throughout the approach, and our faces were close—only divided by the thin lens of Laodicea's eye. Her attire was much like my own, although her curves filled out her ensemble quite differently.

Electroencephalogram, magnetic resonance imaging, and positron emission tomography also prove crucial in pinpointing the origin of Subject R's atonic seizures. Despite the left twin having female genitalia and the right one exhibiting that of a male's—resultant of two of their father's sperm simultaneously fertilizing only one of their mother's eggs, prior to that egg's incomplete division—the subjects are near identical in all other physiological features.

The Eyes, she said through the tube that connected her mouth to my ear, are the windows to Heaven's desire. When we look into them, without touching them, we sustain our own image in them to intensify ourselves through their orbs of obsession. When contact cannot be avoided, we do so enveloped in rubber. Behind these latex integuments, flesh is suppressed from communicating its evil.

It became clear to me that to neutralize her I should twist her erotic obsession into revulsion, to weaponize the angel's eyes towards her fatal and opposite end. Then I, through insidious charms and with a malicious stratagem brewing, spoke to the Fetishist thus:

Ah, I've forgotten so much on my brief sojourn to the shoreline. But do rest assured my flesh has no desire to come into contact with yours—or to let yours touch mine, for that matter. While I was away, my skin, under the auspices of my full-body latex attire, broke out in a rash of bright, blistering angel's eyes.

I showed her my bare hand—avoiding physical contact with the cyclopean eye she inhabited. An allergic reaction of which, without doubt, had developed from prolonged exposure to latex itself. I speculate that Laodicea is plagued too by this aliment. I do understand that the eye which you're

---

Subjects L and R benefit from being able to process concurrent and contrary pieces of information, while each of their physical bodies, which their novel brain-complex controls, can perform contemporaneous and ambidextrous tasks.

holed away in is like all the dolorous others that gaze down from heaven at us, I said, but the lesser clusters of eyes on this island have spread like a wanton infection.

Double, the Fetishist called me, how do you mean that? It was seconds after she'd asked that my plan fully crystalized, and so I paused to give it one last, internal audit before baiting her thus: What I mean is that it's our latex—I'm certain of it—which no longer protects, so much as afflicts. If the dark side effect of ultimate intimacy, achieved through material flesh-to-flesh contact, is parthenogenesis, that rubber suit you're adorned with—which hinders you from the utmost corporeal union with me and our fallen angel—prefers the dark side effect of allergic reaction over true pleasure. We must choose the lesser of two distinct evils. A communion through any means never comes full circle without an incarnate transmission. Lovers who wear the perennial vesicle of the lovers' disease, like spouses bear rings on their fingers, have managed the apical rite of exchange. So, knowing this, rubber on flesh is ever denied sublimation through true love's prevention or mimesis.

Given an advanced handwriting assignment, in which Subjects L and R choose to compose an original story, each body's dominant hand takes on a key role to complete each other's words and sentences in real-time. For instance, if Subject L was beginning any initial half of a desired sentence or word on her left-sided page, within their shared composition book, then Subject R would be completing that sentence or word, in sync with his sister's efforts, on his right-sided page.

Double, she asked with naive yet genuine concern, I bear no symptoms of allergy that I know of. Can my only means of protection turn itself into an imperilment against me as it has done to you?

What I fear, I lied, is that an outbreak is imminent for you—for the eyes are a symptom of overexposure. To prevent this scurge coursing over my body entirely, I waived my plagued hand before her to emphasize reference to it, I had to strip myself bare intermittently.

My tongue is aching to lick them—Laodicea's eyes, she gravely admitted. I don't favor such a position of remove and objectification, but I avoid sinning by keeping my own skin enclosed, barred, and unseen behind this black, shining, rubbery armor.

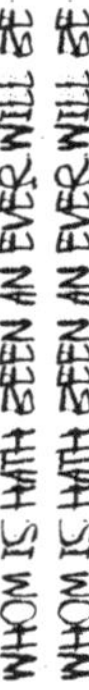

In all truth, Double, I embellished, my tongue is aching as well, not for Laodicea's eyes, but for your own. She twisted her body around within the cyclopean eye, pressing her backside towards me, against its transparent cornea. This was the Fetishist's invitation to a sensual play in which our wanton bodies would bring one another to climax without touching skin. I reciprocated—grinding my groin into her rubber-clad ass. Despite our exoskeletal, onyx encasements and the thick, transparent cornea be-

---

The level of synchronicity and simultaneity which Subjects L and R demonstrate throughout this assignment give strong indication to either a shared or singular consciousness.

tween us, there was a profundity of sensa-
tion to be had. I caressed her spine up to
her shoulders until she'd twisted herself in
the eye-pus to face me. The Fetishist managed just fine, massaging my unexposed cock
through the slickwet, transparent boundary.

Dare to find a way in here with me, she teased.
I feigned a recoil in order make myself ever
so slightly out of her reach. Extreme mea-
sures were needed to move my plans forward. I pressed my bare many-eyed palm
to the transparent cornea which she stood
behind. My palm and its surface instantly
sizzled on contact. Laodicea's central eye
dented under my influence as a new rash
of eyes spread up my arm and over the rest
of my body, under the coverage of latex.

Angel eyes blistered themselves into being
and opened new windows into my secret desires, over my elbows, across my chest, within the concavities of my armpits, up my neck,
along my cheek and forehead, upon my lips,
and at the tip of my tongue. I bit down on
the eyeball my tongue had become—letting
my infectious blood drain down into the dark
inner lumen of the tube that served as a con-
duit between my mouth and the Fetishist's
ear. I could only assume that it reached her
because she was shaking in sudden hysterics
and screaming: Trickster! Leprous, lecher-

The fragmentary construction of the twins' texts may seem unusually cryptic; yet, once pieced together, their writings read with striking linearity. Regardless of their documents' peculiarities, when compared side-by-side, these bizarrelly constructed half-texts do yield, at least, an intelligible tale.

ous trickster! What have you done with my double, and what have you done now to me?

There coursed a great tremor under my body, and the central eye's blood vessels ruptured. Its buckling cornea cracked and caved in, imploding all but the socket. The Fetishist and I fell to the base of the pit of simmering eye gore. She padded my fall, and I lay atop her. I wrestled her rubber-lined body, grappling her in the gore-laden shallows. I told her I'd want an intimate moment with her, before making her into a corpse. I removed the two tubes connecting us at our masks. She promptly sealed off her exposed ear and lips with corresponding zippers. I did the same for the sake of etiquette. I simply wanted for us to be able to move against one another—a slickwet latex embrace without the risk of my flesh abrading or bruising her own. With each sliding stroke of my rubber-gloved hand, each kiss from my latex-bound lips to hers, my excitement intensified, and I finally understood the appeal of it all as she struggled to free herself from me. This obstructed form of touch could be magnified without making its pleasures unbearable to the especially sensitive.

I continued exploring the Fetishist's curves with deep and amorous petting. My single ungloved hand, ruinous as it was in its want

---

The 46-page document, provided above, is an unabridged transcription of the twins' handwritten story—which is apparently rooted in the gnostic myths of their former faith (not endorsed by this study's administrators).

to bring ruin, was slyly caressing her nape while feeling around for her habit's back zipper. And when my eye-plagued fingers had found it, I fully unzipped the Fetishist—forcefully spinning her body around to tear her out bare by her hair from the back of her latex attire. She was a moist, softened, insectile mulatto, prematurely pried out from her exoskeletal sheath. With my evil hand crushing her breast, holding her down to be washed in the shallows, baptizing her in our socket of carnage, the Fetishist's once flawless, ecru complexion was consumed head to toe in blistering eyes. Although she fought back and futilely tried to resist it, all that had flowered upon her would soon bloat and burst from the eyes' high volatility and her overexposure. I let go, gave her the space to stand up on her own—a stuttering carcass mutilated by eyes. Subjugated by me, her alleged double, diseased and repulsed by the object of her desire, the Fetishist had been transposed: her fetish delivered both her and itself into a common repugnance.

I could hear you again, somewhere within the left of my mind. You'd been theorizing that the island-sized angel's reawakening was in some way a symbiotic retaliation to the Fetishist's brutal demise. By the time the island's once-flaccid talons and wings slapped the ocean in death throes, the Fetishist's con-

Under scrutiny, having already been rigorously indoctrinated into the creeds of their parents' former religion, Subjects L and R insist (in simpler terms) that an inherit theophany can be drawn from decoding their story—implying that their above text is a written manifestation of some divine agency.

quered flesh looked as though thousands of bullets passed through her. Victoriously, I clambered out of Laodicea's socket. Every parasite eye on the island began to balloon out beyond its capacity. Every last pupil appeared ripe to rupture with sputters of serous and pus. Like some aspiring Iscariot, I delighted among all the agony in the garden of eyes. I stepped out to Laodicea's coast, between one of its furious wings and a neighboring talon. I undressed—my skin rendered rugged by legions of eyes—and dove into the cleansing saline of the ocean. You gave me the needed directions in order to reach the next island. You said that I moved like Mercurius over the water, but I corrected you—knowing that both he and mercury were much denser than water and would've moved under it rather than over it if he had tried. You had nothing to say in rebuttal. What I wish you had told me, however, was that Thyatira, the next island over, could've been reached without actually swimming to it. I exerted myself for no reason or gain. You giggled within the left side of my brain as I made this a point of contention. Perhaps it was you who was more like Mercurius, some kind of quicksilver trickster—leading me towards an end marred with hubris and utter despair.

Thyatira was a sprawling necropolis made wholly from mirrored glass. A monotonous

FLICK
FLO
BLO
TELEVI
ANNOU
FAKE
FLE
PRUR.
MAL
INSEC
AN

Yet, what their tale amounts to, under a less fanatical lens, is a linguistically idiosyncratic parable that, much like their shared bodies in relation to their coupled minds, has become indissociable from the subjects' actual worldview.

MADE TO FUNCTION LIKE SOME WEAPON NERVES

unpeopled city of chromium sepulchers. All I needed to do, as you'd been helpful enough to allude to, was to see my reflection within any of its surfaces to advance myself across its architectures. And so, looking up at its jagged mirror-glass shores, from sea level, below it, I found my reflection within them; and, so, just like that, I was already there on its coast. After getting used to this way of traveling via reflection, I arrived at the gates beyond which its cemetery of mirrors extended. I had no need to move—for as long as I found my own image on some distant reflective structure, be it a mirror-glass crucifix, mausoleum, tombstone, saintly effigy, or cenotaph, I'd be transported. My body would bend and contort uncannily whenever turning each vertices' corners or curves. Since casting off the previous island's required attire, my body roamed naked again. In mirrors, I watched the parasite eyes on my skin desiccate and scab over, a hundred or more at a time, flaking off and dissipating. I looked rather hairless and pale, having ridden myself of them.

You suggested I pause in my journey, to take solace and time in the absence of conflict to reflect upon something both relevant and specific: the divine metaphor of mirror and shadow. Feeling supreme in my arrogance and ambition, I shrugged off your unsought advice. You asked if I only had love for my

---

While collaborative writing, as a medium, serves as a mediator between any two parties in dialog—collaborative writing, as an analog to direct transcosmic exchange is perhaps too pataphysical to be considered within the agnostic scope of this exercise.

triumphs and conquests; I was quick to affirm your suspicions. You insinuated that if
we were ever to meet one another in person,
we'd be driven to love or to hate at first sight.
I still wasn't sure that your voice was more
than imagined. You spoke of having a body,
that of a beautiful woman with sleek, hairless skin, the shade and sheen of mahogany.

You spoke of the Lucent, the third of the
Seven Enigmas, having duplicitous powers, abilities to reflect artifice rather than
merely the thing that its mirror flesh sees.
You guided me, as I requested, towards a curious body of light—certain that this was the
one called the Lucent. It was important, you
had insisted, that I decouple—shadow from
body, body from shadow—prior to facing
this adversary. So, complying, I placed full
awareness inside of my shadow and left my
body to cast itself underneath it—deigned to
serve as a shadow of its own shadow. Towing my flesh in the background, my umber
proclaimed itself sovereign over the foreground. As shadow I could expand and contract at whim and blacken each mirror which
I'd project into or out from. By the time
I'd closed in upon the Lucent, I'd shrouded
one half of the island's reflective necropolis.

The half I hadn't yet darkened was blindingly bright—the luminous work of the

---

*Once this conclusion was drawn, a transcript of the
twins' work was printed and promptly faxed over to
a satellite testing laboratory to be reviewed and interpreted by a similar study group, openly affiliated with
the Church.*

YOUR BLOODSTARVED WANT AN YOUR HUNGRY SCALPELS AN YOUR SEXUAL
THEE LUMINOUS VIOLENCE THAT EXTOLS US AN WE WILL SUCK FULL ON BODY

Lucent. I stood face to face with this being and, starving for this confrontation, attempted to suck all its radiance cold. Yet, as I did so, my own umber brightened and faded. I nigh-disappeared before giving up on the light that I could not contain. The Lucent was no longer darkened by me. Its humanoid figure was naturally featureless—a malleable, smooth, and gleaming integument of reflective chromium skin. With a finger, the Lucent traced its midsagittal plane, demarcating itself with a line or inclusion from the base of its sexless groin to the top of its faceless head. Half of my physical body was then reflected at me within the sharp bounds of its leftward hemisphere. The reflection of half of another, a bald, brown-skinned woman, appeared on the right. You swore that her likeness, literally, was the splitting image of yours. Only the chromium eyes, teeth, and mucosa of each of these hemispherical beings would differentiate them from ourselves. I was taken aback, and accidentally let some of the light I'd consumed leak from my shadowy contours.

The Lucent took back the rays I had stolen from it—inhaling them into the nuclear glare of its eyes, enhancing the sheen of its flesh which wore the reflection of said bisexual

---

It's been suggested that the subjects' additional corpus callosum, which both conjoins them and serves as an intermediary bundle of neurons, allows the two brains to function as one larger unit or system. However, in terms of self-reference, the subjects' interchangeable use of plurality and singularity puts any particular theory (regarding their likely unique understanding of selfhood) into question.

creature. I let my accompanying body take over, wind up his fist, and strike at the Lucent's glass jaw. My body nursed himself—plucking mirror glass shards from his crimson wet knuckles with only his milky white teeth. I looked up to admire what damage he'd caused to the Lucent. The jaw had been shattered, and the Lucent's firm poise broken. Its gynandromorphed face had been marred by the instance of blunt trauma injury—my blood loss smeared over its illusory, bisexual features. Yet none of the impact was lasting. The jaw realigned and restored itself to its former perfection. The hemisphere that held my likeness then faded, and what took its place was the other half of the hairless mahogany woman—completing your alleged form in its mirror. Virtual rather than corporeal—a nonetheless ravishing mirage of the you who both was and wasn't—your vitality represented in every shining inch of the Lucent's refracted skin.

The woman—or, for all intents and purposes, you—a darkling emanating from the light, and my self—a pale shade of umbrage—evaluated each other, growling synchronically like rival ferals. Locking gazes, we backed away in our mutual field of uncomfortable closeness. I found your image most compelling in the desert of reflective

---

Previous split-brain experiments on felines, chimpanzees, and humans, wherein a corpus callosotomy was performed, were crucial in the identification of operative differences between the two hemispheres. After surgically severing the corpus callosum, the left and right sides of the brain would then function independently of one another.

tombs, where the winds howled as if we and this desolate place were its chimes, where we doubtlessly shared the swirling vibrations that rattled the cemetery as much as our teeth, where you nonetheless hid behind quavering graves in the childish hope that I'd seek you. And I saw my shadow fluttering upon each shuddering gravestone as I did so, as if the wisdom and vanity of those mirrored graves were showing me that my choice of action, in seeking, was utterly grave. When I'd finally found you, or your likenesses at least, I made myself known just long enough for her to witness my shadow recede behind the fine line where the cenotaphs were shrouded in shade on one side and reflecting bright light on the unshrouded other. And whenever she'd find me, her chromium teeth would gleam savage when smiling. In the line that divided our playing field, she'd prop herself up on a headstone. Spreading her legs and realigning them in a way that evoked the sacred profanity of organismic geometry, she, the artifice of the Lucent, emanated venereal brilliance—rays shooting out from her chromium sex into the silhouette of my swelling genital plexus. My body's pale sex hardened to spatter

---

Most fascinating of all is the difference in side-effects which arose between humans and other animal species. While split-brain surgeries enabled cats and monkeys to retain twice as much information, bisecting the hemispheres of humans' brains demonstrated that the left side could interpret language, while the right hemisphere, following corpus callosotomy, could not. Furthermore, humans who had previously undergone surgery could not compare stimuli across their two visual fields, since visual processing is primarily right-brained.

WE MUST REGAIN THAT GNOSIS WE HATH LOST

the tomb where her legs splayed across it. Pearlescent cum swirled with my shadow's bituminous ichor. Three of her mahogany fingers pushed past her stretched labia into her chromium gash. In the anticipation of climax, I tightened the grip on the selfhood I favored and struck at the mirror-glass floor. The Lucent came down from her tombstone, equally wanton and giddy with fear. Squatting beside me, she beat at the floor as I had. Bloodied glass shards and mirror dust fragments—her fist as balled up and damaged as mine was. Together, our injuries dug a moderate hole into the shattered reflective glass floor. We'd expected to find a vast cache of skeletons plated in chromium mirror. Yet what we'd uncovered seethed out, fumes rising from the underground's cloud of unknowing. Staring into its penumbral, unnervingly neutral, nonsensical exhalations, we anxiously shoveled the glass dust and large jagged shards back over the source of escape.

I'd been previously familiarized with that substance, knowing well that this cloud of unknowing, if given the chance to surround us within its gray, sense-purging vapors, would nullify our staunch antonymous stances as well as disqualify either of us from achieving divinity's stature. Despite our swift cover-up, the breach in the mirror-glass floor started spreading. Between the distinct delineation of our territorial dark-

---

It remains the chief goal of this pilot abscission to alleviate Subject L , at least, from the symptoms of Subject R's atonic episodes.

ness and light a chasm branched out from those cracks, eager to lengthen and widen. It threatened to split the whole island in two and prevent divine opposites from uniting.

A billowing and expansive cloud of unknowing belched forth from its fathomless depths. Unlike the end goal of the dual reality that surrounded us, its churning penumbra had come to subsume any truth, whether alternate or absolute, which dared to defy it—a cannibal of and from pure abyss, born from neither shadow nor mirror, horrifically crawling and gaseous. It spread across and consumed more and more from the center, thus splitting the island in two. Upon the inadvertent reflection of its gray hue, the Lucent succumbed to collapse under subliminal inundation (delivering neither visceral nor cosmic torment, but an intimate, if uncoscious, torment regardless). Seeing the Lucent writhe in such transcendental and epigenetically raw saddled pain, knowing it had been edged to this unraveled state by the cloud of unknowing between us, my shadow drank full on its light's emissions to further it towards certain self-harm and destruction. This inflamed my body's red gums with the sting of unspeakable glee. Across the chasm, where the cloud of unknowing had not yet seethed above, I watched as your reflection lost her fixity and composure. Poorly superimposed on the mirror-flesh of the Lucent, she squirmed in lust's agony un-

---

Prior to their pre-operative preparations for surgical separation, it is decided that the twins' individual visual fields should be tested.

til she no longer could. Her chromium gash, lacking its typical luster, come-hithered me, and I, lacking pity, denied her. From that distance I thought that she couldn't, but her chromium fingernails beamed vindictive with a light that managed to penetrate—boring injurious holes in my shadow. The bedazzling reach that the Lucent had over mine was a crafty beguilement in itself. Just to defeat it, I lapped up its light as if I were addicted to it. So, I looked over its long provocative rays, laid out before me like glinting white lines of cocaine. I saw myself snorting it up through a shadowy nostril. Enamored with that pulchritudinous image, of the you which the Lucent had conjured for me that, from one instance and onto the next, interchanged us as charmer and charmed.

And in that line of thinking, whenever she'd scintillate, beads of her chromium menstrual blood sparkling, I'd loom in as shadow to darken and mix with the wholly enchanting illusory glow—considering, if for but a moment, the possibility that, if united and synchronized, despite our perspective from shadow to mirror, we might achieve, if conjoined and collegial, a fine state of Godhead together. Initially we, your reflection, my body, and my shadow, would sit across from the other at the edges of the chasm to dip our feet in its cloud of unknowing—allowing our toes to dissipate in its anesthetic, ambiguous nether. And we'd echo its infinite gluttony in our stimulus-starved and vacuous pupils. As the

------

To do this, Subject L's mouth is first to be gagged, and Subject R's eyes are first to be blindfolded.

LIVING AS THOUGH THEY HATH DIED GUIDES

chasm gaped wider so waned our proximity.

We took this, however, as a cruel opportuni-ty to further torture our presumably mutual feelings, our impossible passions, and unre-quited amours. The Lucent would radiate heat in the insatiable peak of your reflection's estrus. My body licked its own semen clean off its hands after seeing its feminine coun-terpart swallow her own cum and menses.

The Lucent experimented with other simi-lar dualist endeavors—making the sign of the cross so that the symbol would trigger trans-figuration via subliminal code. As a response to this sign, my own shadow was humbled into the shape of a crucifix, with my body mirroring it—face-down on a looking-glass field, pressing into its tera quisquilia. Hu-miliated and raging, my shadow attempted to cast a measure of shade at the halogen halo hovering over your reflection's chro-mium clitoris, but the strobing magnificence of the halo's electromagnetic corona inspired within me such rapturous seizures that I was convinced I'd succumb to untimely conces-sions—my martyrdom at the Lucent's dispos-al. With each consecutive seizure, the chasm further extended across the mirror-glass floor. From its side of the split in the cemetery, the shimmering Lucent ceased baiting me with your mimic because it had whittled away at

---

Being able to see, yet unable to speak, Subject L is in-structed to draw one card for her brother from a pre-shuf-fled deck of the Smith-Waite tarot. The card which she draws for her brother is that of the Two (II) of Swords, the signifier of a powerful division of allegiance.

UL FORGET THAT WE HAD DONE WITH THATGAME

enough of my umber's density and depth to diminish my silhouette fully—its chromium mirror-flesh beaming malicious delight.

My attention had been diverted as the last of the gravestones, crosses, saintly effigies, mausoleums, and cenotaphs tipped over the floor's widely-unpursing lips and down into the throat of a gray, gaseous abyss. The chasm became so enlarged that there was little mirror-glass left to either side of the island. Much of the power we'd held over the other was weakened by distance. I reenveloped myself in my shadow, and the reflective skin of the Lucent occulted itself in an armor of light—our hidden features forgotten within these less vulnerable archetypes. For as long as I could, I adopted the tone of the night with an air of deliberate, sensual indifference. I cared to appear to the Lucent as utterly cold, impenetrably dark, and uncaring in order to drain and then dim its barely approachable brightness. Before the Lucent—the first among us to lose footing—took its graceless plunge into the chasm and into the cloud of unknowing, it flickered a brief, final tease of your hairless mahogany image. It was baiting me, obviously, to go diving in after it.

A voice, now with your stunning figure and features assigned, you'd fallen silent in me for long enough that I'd come to wonder if you'd escaped from the left of my skull through an ear hole, if you'd gone mum by sheer jealousy at my alchemistry with your reflection contrived by the Lucent, or if you'd merely been a delusion I'd finally overcome. I thought, say something, say anything, as the last of the mirror-glass floor began to deteriorate, and I too was losing my footing. Perhaps the cloud of unknowing had bested us all. I let myself go with my shadow in the lead. It was like sinking rather than diving. I envisioned myself as Mercurius—heavier, obviously, than the cloud—hunting the tail of a light streak, bypassing the gloom and all its penumbral annulments for selfish and umbral eclipses. When my shadow caught up to the Lucent, I was too eager to gobble its glow—an open black cloak lunging towards light, engorging myself upon the mirror-fleshed Lucent's smooth, featureless form. The Lucent tried to diminish my shade, but I absorbed each of its offensive rays—vampirizing the halo of light that had failed to protect the Lucent. From the two holes in the mirror-flesh, wherein my shadow sank its bituminous fangs, the Lucent bled out its heart's liquid chromium blood. In the thick of the cloud of unknowing, mirror and shadow, the competitive archetypes coveting lightness and darkness, defused. My

---

When escorted into the operatory, the teens throw a short-lived, emotionally charged, albeit physically nonviolent tantrum. Only once they have exhausted themselves are they lifted onto the surgical table and administered nitrous oxide, followed by general anesthesia.

body was nullified by this penumbra as well.

My final thoughts were of you, your illusory image, your toned, feminine, sheen, and hairless mahogany skin, and the chromium tongue that had come from your mimic's plush lips—gratifyingly kissing the heart of my darkness. I sucked you into my silhouette, where I could savor your secrets. After that whole ordeal, I'd gone comfortably numb and forgetful. I only knew what I'd stated up to this point because you were there on the other side of the cloud of unknowing, waiting to promptly remind me. For the very first time, I heard you calling my name from outside of my skull—urging me to awaken. My left eyelid opened; my right eyelid didn't. My body was dealing with general right-sided weakness. I'd asked you if I'd had a stroke. I'd been propped up within an upright glass coffin in a curious place you informed was the sole visitor's hall to the Museum of Alchemical Marriage. It was an expansive, one-story rotunda without any obvious entrance or exit—an entire facility which encompassed Ephesus, taking up the whole of that anciently sunken land. Glass-housed dioramas were displayed to the right of me, and a handrail was fixed to my left. You suggested I steady my gait with the handrail. A black wall of opaqueness stood right behind the transparent coffin. To reach the opposite side of it I would have to traverse the tubular hall counterclockwise All other walls were transparent. To the left,

---

Conjoined sister and brother lose consciousness while in a four-armed embrace.

the deep, desolate sea could be viewed. The ceilings and the floors were tiled in bas reliefs depicting old wars between Catholics and Cathars. There were no chandeliers; the only luminous sources came from within the right side's dimly lit dioramas. This singular hall had been shaped like a hoop, and, from an aerial view, its roof crafted to resemble a serpent devouring its tail while constricting the ripe, cosmic egg—thus, the museum's natural history displays, confined to that large rotunda's ovoid center, represented the egg which the hallway—suggestive of the ouroboros—encircled. This eccentric, however thoughtful, construction was all a design of the Lover's. She, the Lover, chief overseer of the Museum of Alchemical Marriage, had resided for ages within. Incidentally, you told me I was now ready to meet you in person, and that you were waiting for me at the terminus of the hall.

Just as before, I was hairless and naked, and I was reminded of my stark-naked intentions directed at God—the one whom I'd come to replace once I'd conquered all Seven Enigmas. You asked if I still referred to myself as the Hater, since, after passing beyond the cloud of unknowing, I'd lost sense of that hate and required reminding in order to simulate all the hatred I'd managed to cultivate prior.

Separation surgery is performed—splitting the fibrous bundle of neurons connecting their brains. It is the duty of science to dismiss the insistence of metaphor, and, so, it will be overlooked that this separation may very well bring absolute ruin to the very first human representation of the supernatural reconciliation of both spirit and matter.

This place, seldom visited, was cobwebbed in self-aware anomie and obsolescence. The tiled floors were caked with mildew and dust and peppered with rust-rotten limbs of odd, disassembled, windup automatons—former residents of the museum who'd served in custodial roles. It would've been dreadful to see them maintaining this place in its prime. Each possessed a soulless, cracked porcelain head with two faces—one in the front and the other, to either the left or the right of it. These monstrous minions skittered the halls on four legs. And they'd four spindly arms for dusting the railings and walls with their four articulate hands—all the while formally dressed in the outfits of butlers and maids. Fucking abominable. Not one of them, praise the **Lord**, was wandering the hallway. They were defunct; I was alone—well, relatively. Your voice carried well from the end of the corridor. You served as my guide, directing my functional left eye to the first diorama to appear at my right side. Neglect had befallen its plastic botanical garden, gray-coated in soot—wilting as if it once lived—under the malnourishment of a dying halogen light.

Within that apocryphal garden was an intricate showcase of gynandromorphic insects, boasting an exquisitely rare and eclectic collection of dual-gendered beetles and butterflies. The male hemispheres were distinct

---

The operation is partly successful insofar as the twins, having been placed in separate recovery rooms, awakening to novel senses of being. However, the surgery has allowed for the manifestation of other adverse, unforeseeable side-effects.

WE WERE CAREER SCIENTISTS EMPLOYED AS

from their feminine halves, intricately patterned and brightly colored on one side while drab and gray on the other—the masculine halves presenting with horns or other ornamental protuberances, with the female halves lacking these morphological characteristics. Some were glued down to appear as though perching on plastic branches and leaves; others were posed with their jaws or proboscises piercing fake flowers—dangling from nigh invisible wires to help them appear as if doing so mid-flight. From the false, painted sky on the diorama's ceiling, hanging from similar wires, were both a full moon and a sun.

Gazing sublimely upon them, from the dead center of this diorama, was a two-headed humanoid angel. On the left was a masculine face whose head was crowned by a kingly wreath. On the right was a female visage—her head crowned as well, but by a queenly tiara. Its left wing was white, and its right wing was red. Its left hand held a shield, and its feminine right hand was clutching an egg. You told me that this was an antiquated display and that, despite what the alchemists thought, contrasting pairs didn't require the other. You said to truly love something was to see it as God, perfected, even if it remained independent and decoupled from its diametric opposite. Unconditional hatred, in turn, was demonstrated by imposition—forcing

---

While it is reasonable to assume that each teen would be able to function independently following the operation, they present the cognitive and dissociative impairments that patients subjected to a full split-brain procedure can, however infrequently, be at risk of.

MATHEMATICAL PHILOSOPHERS STONES THAT

WE DIVIN ANU THEN SEPA HIG MEAS FROM FU HALLUCI OF ASCE ANCI

WE NOT INCOMPLETION OF COMPLETENESS ULTIMATE THEE ILLUMINATE AN BEWARE WILL

a union or harmony with any being who'd
rather resist it. I saw precisely where you
were going with this, even though I didn't
agree with your system. It was the operating
philosophy of the Lover's and one which I'd
come to despise. With only my left leg to
stand on, I had no choice but to hop, going
forward—my left hand gripping the left-sided railing to bolster and balance myself.

My right leg was dragging, the right arm
limp at my side. I hadn't completely lost
feeling in them. I couldn't let this concern
me. If I could locate the Lover and subsume her, I'd advance onward: to the next
island, against the next Enigma; whether
on Pergamum, Smyrna or Sardis—once far
from this place, I'd surely be fine. Prag-
matically, I hobbled as best as I could. 

Carefully stepping around the funereal heaps
of decommissioned custodians—noting the
nigh-erogenous postures into which they'd
slumped before their winders stopped winding, cogs jamming in motionless clockwork.
Some were frozen in agonized estrus, others entwined in obscene combinations of
simultaneous coition and brutal assault.
Their machine parts were partially hidden by torn and moth-ridden uniforms.

Most of their synthetic skin had long since
rotted away—save for the odd fleshy el-

---

*Upon her first post-op exam, Subject L demonstrates
slightly more mental stability in comparison to her brother. She is no longer suffering from atonic episodes that
continue to hinder Subject R.*

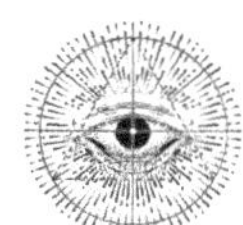

bow or shin—and even those remnants were pocked and cankered by time. With a modicum of caution, hopping over rag-doll carcasses, I browsed the museum's other life-sized vivariums—where were housed the frayed and forgotten examples of taxidermic chimeras, lifeless and stilted, free from all pathologic concern. In the second dim window I peered through, I'd found an utterly enigmatic, yet otherwise implausible, union: a relegated lion's head fused to the proportionate tail of a serpent—its frozen expression, forever exhibiting regal pride and ferocity while ironically fixed in its taxidermic imprisonment. With large sections of every display obscured by the grit of that gallery's age, the mythical beasts these enclosed were only partly revealed—leaving a lingering puzzlement in the stale air surrounding these strange and mystical animal hybrids of awesome and measureless charm.

When confronting the next in this series of dioramas, you suggested I peak through small windows of cleanliness in the filth covered glass from across where I stood. I spied on the dignified skeletons of centaurs, standing fully erect on the sands of a mock-coastal setting; two territorial cynocephalic dogmen squabbled below a verdant forest canopy; a doe-eyed goatfish basked in idyllic abandon upon the synthesized bluffs of a lakeshore; white cattle with womanly faces suckled

---

Since the seizures had not originated in Subject L's brain and the connection between hers and his has been severed, she will no longer receive any oncoming signals between her own brain and that of her brother's.

each other's milk-spewing udders, some swapping white fluid from mouth to mouth within their engoldened, inanimate pasture.

There were seemingly endless stretches of more-of-the-same chimeric displays. I wouldn't quite say that I was becoming fatigued by the tedium of it all but limping along proved increasingly strenuous. The further I limped, my right arm and leg advanced in atrophy. I kept a keen eye up ahead on the continuous curve of the hall—hopping laboriously on my left leg as my entire right side continued to shrivel. Even then, it was unbelievable that a person could live with only one hemisphere left to their body.

By the time that I reached a novel exhibit, my entire right side had receded. I existed solely from my midsagittal line to my left side. To my right, there remained tissue tags—barely prominent enough to even be classified as vestigial. There was less weight to bear now, at least. I found it disturbingly comforting that the rest of my body caught up to match the inherent deformity in my sternum (as I had mentioned, I had been born, yet again and again, with only the left-sided half of it). When I'd brought up the matter while rounding the hallway, you reiterated a stance you'd had from the start: The sternum, you said, from your end of the

Subject L's brain continues to swell, following surgery; her scalp has stretched beyond its capacity, and there is concern that both it and her skull might soon shatter and burst from the pressure. She claims to hear the fragmented voice of her brother inside of her head and seems extremely distressed about what he is saying to her.

hall, is like the clay seal of a covenant made with oneself. When the sternum is evenly split down the midline or—in your case, congenitally missing—one half of its anatomical whole, it can be paired to the half of another who is missing the opposing side. Thus, what you have within you is part of a symbolon—a fragment of the divine key needed in order to conjugate an inherently broken relationship. Should you arrive at the end of my hall without the knowledge required to do this, I will still love you regardless...

Your last phrase echoed especially, clarifying your role in my serial labors. In order to best interblend with a lover, I'd have to revert myself back to the Hater. I had the potential to be one, no doubt, but I hadn't the motive. You'd come to my aid on countless occasions within this, my anagogic pilgrimage. And, while your tendency to one-sided communication was frustrating, you seldom left me clueless when crucial hints were needed to make progress. I'd reserve my hatred until whenever we'd next meet. The only thing I might have loathed was God in Heaven and Their continual refusal to incorporate me into Them. You were just as far from God and as equally opposed to Them as I was. Together we'd accomplished so much through subverting Them. You'd proved yourself to be a comrade, not an adversary. I thought no more on this. Eventually, I came to the last of the dioramas. This one was well-lit, shin-

---

Subject R's seizures have only increased. He's been rendered incapable of actual speech and language comprehension.

393

ing as brightly as it did because the dust encrusted display glass had been ravaged previously with large, jagged portions bashed out from the window into it and shattered on the flooring elsewhere. And I could piece together all the evidence therein to draw conclusions as to why this vandalism happened. This vivarium was dedicated to Mercurius; it said so on the placard. And the iconography, while torn asunder, confirmed this.

I assumed, given what remained of its key elements, that the taxidermied God of Thieves himself was meant to be positioned standing on a large and ancient ovum of stone, holding his caduceus in one hand and the planetary glyph of sulfur on a crosier in the other. He'd originally been attended on each flank by two taxidermied male nobles, all of which, Mercurius included, were now gutted and dismembered on the floor. The ovum of stone had been smashed open, and the incubating serpent—which it no longer cradled within—had been stomped and flattened. Mercurius and his attendants, torn in two above their waists, had bled out wood-wool stuffing across the base of their terrarium. Slumped over them were two pathetic custodian automatons.

The cracks along their porcelain faces rendered their intended features and expressions indiscernible. One wore a Victorian maid's dress, the other a butler's black livery. Both

---

It is almost as if, now divided, the two have become maladapted as literal halfwits—each sibling functioning as if just one side of their respective brains' work.

moth-worn outfits had been modified to accommodate their extra limbs. The windup levers which jutted from their backs—which needed to be cranked in order to reanimate them—had rusted to a halt some time ago.

I surmised there'd been a failed mutiny on behalf of the automatons of this museum. I wondered if they'd gotten to you too—for I was at least certain these custodial automatons depended on you for continual assistance; to wind them up, to commission them, to give them purpose, to keep them functioning.

See, as I had said, you're just like Mercurius, I heard you say again. There was layered truth to it—especially in that torn state that he and I were in. And to obtain his lapis philosophorum—the cosmic egg, which this exhibit represented—I'd do anything. Whether that required trickery or thieving, treachery, or total transformation, I was as game for it now as I had been previously. You are almost near, just a little further, you encouraged me. I could see the black wall at the end from this distance—the other side of it from where I'd started. And I could see, leaning upright on that wall, the clear glass coffin which you stood in, awaiting me. And I could also see the left side of your body torn asunder on the tiles where the rioting automatons that did you in sucumbed to pre-

---

Reintroduced under close supervision, Subject L attacks Subject R at the first opportunity. Had she not been restrained precisely midway through the act she might have gone through with gauging out Subject R's eyes with her thumbs.

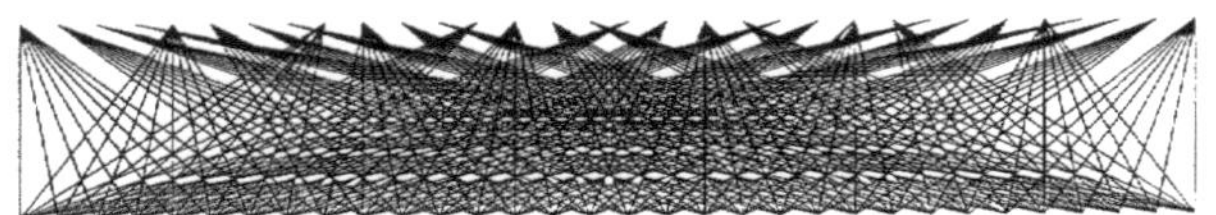

mature inanimation over it. And I could see
the half of you which managed to continue
standing in defiance, mummified by ancient,
insurrectionary violence—your hairless,
once-mahogany skin embalmed in years of
dust. And I could see, through desiccated
flesh, the outline of your partial sternum.
Your right hemisphere, reposed in death, offered a compatible, appealing, optimal ant-
onymy. Your corpse, however, did not seem
as though it was still capable of speech. Then
I saw it—clenched between your half-arch of
opalescent teeth—a tiny, amplified speaker.

MARTYRED
CHRIS

Your voice projected from it: Have you the
knowledge needed to bring utter telos or,
at least, semblance to our missing pieces?

THEOLOGY
STUD

I'll conjoin our bodies; we'll become a novel rebis and dethrone the Godhead—simultaneously bound in life and death, in love
and hate, in ripeness and decay, I offered.

TO BE
MORE

Love, you retorted, wishes to be free from
any bondage, and I have come to love us
as we've been and will be. Yet, I don't
want to lose what's left of us—to let that
be subsumed into some transcendental
thing, some volatile, temporary whole.

SURGICAL
FETIS
THAN ONES

Extracting piecemeal answers from our con-
versation was becoming tediously difficult

*When asked what she'd hoped to accomplish through vi-
olence, Subject L stated that she believed that her twin
brother's expanding and unwelcome presence within the
limited space in her head was the cause of her worsening
encephalitis and that only through murdering him could
she be awarded relief.*

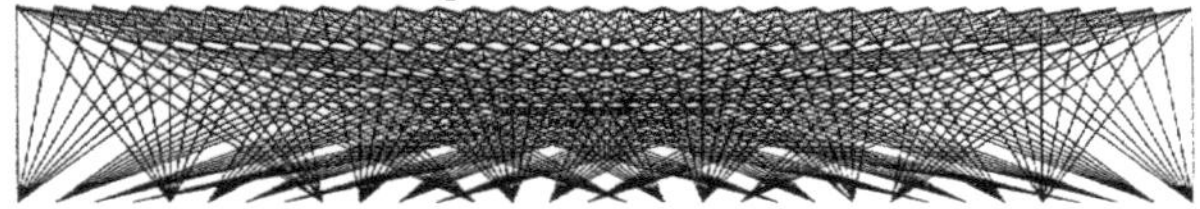

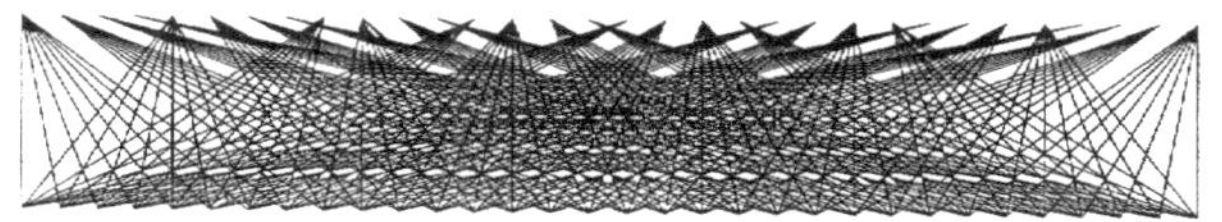

to manage. I became impatient and irate. I asked the following question in a way that matched my current passions: Are you implying that the state of godliness is temporary?

Attaining godhood was your goal, not mine, you admitted with an undertone of coyness. Perhaps it was unfair of me to never state my aim, but what I've always wanted was an everlasting love for you and I, one that allocates for one another's independence and considerately offers space and distance.

But what I counter-offered with was considerate. It was, in fact, the absolute, the unconditional, an ultimatum. What you, the Lover, were subscribing to was nothing but a double standard, a love not boundless, yet binding, and conditional—no matter how 'considerate' you swore it was. I was finished with this abhorrent exchange of rhetoric. I pondered where exactly you were speaking from. Your voice, if not drawn out from within my mind, if not coming from within your corpse—if what I had been looking at, within your clear glass coffin, was in fact your corpse and not another's.

I doubted everything you'd told me up to that point. I scanned your moth-begotten, mummified cadaver—there was something glistening within your dried right socket,

According to her, any attempted negotiations with him would prove futile, as Subject R could no longer communicate in that alleged, unspoken language which they had once shared. Further testing, therapy sessions, and other remedial interventions were offered, yet Subject L has since become belligerent and non-complaint.

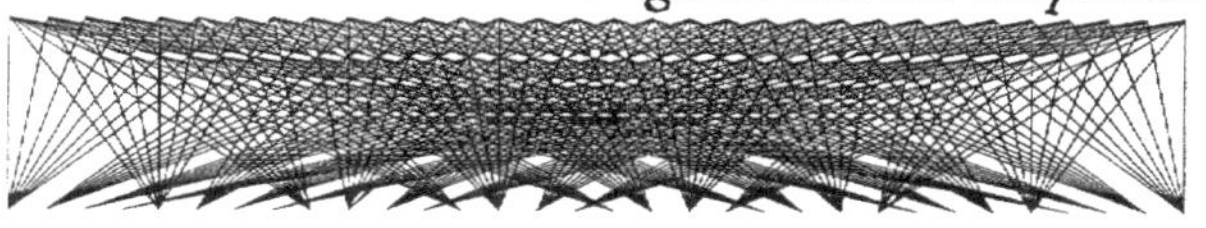

IS IT ~~BY~~ GODS WILL THAT TWIN SIBLINGS ENG

some kind of glossy aperture or camera lens had been embedded where the eye had been. I could not confirm what I was seeing from this distance. I needed to get closer, but in the act of closing the distance I sensed that every effort I'd been spewing forth within this damnable museum was being chronicled, recorded—not merely for the purpose of monitoring but with the intention of examining my nuances upon some remote large-scale screen, to make a rare exhibit of me.

I was done with words; they'd failed me. Within the limitations I was forced to work with I made haste to confront you physically. Yet in the midst of nearing your cadaver, the railing made a 'snapping' sound before it gave out under my left hand. I fell flat on my right side—my smoothed-out plane of flesh aligning parallel upon the cold and moldy floor tiles. I was facing you, but you were too far from my reach—as was anything around me. My limbs were useless in this situation.

Was I wrenched by irony in this moment of arrest, or had my fate been plotted? Your gentle voice attempted to address my circumstance through that small speaker in your mouth, but my surge of growling hatred for you muted it. My plans to overcome you were collapsing, as were my dreams of leaving the

---

Similarly, Subject R is too disoriented and despondent for any of those remedies to be effective. The ill-disposed state in which these formally conjoined teens have been left in has led to violent and ceaseless disputes between their once-intimate parents.

REST BROTHERS THAT WILL GROW FROM US

Museum of Alchemical Marriage, the island of Ephesus, and the ocean it had sunken in, were dissipating like a sun-scorched vapor.

I'd thought, at least, that my internal monologues would be enough to drown you out, but I was wrong. The aperture lodged inside the hollow socket of your corpse gazed down upon me like all apertures of Heaven had. From your speaker you broke through my wallowing:

All things that I've collected here are those I cherish most. Everything stays lovely in its solitary place. The moths might gnaw at us, and the dust might pile on, but nothing will corrupt the love-display that we'll put on.

I thought about the fabulous assassination plots I had reserved for the one called the Salvager on the floating landfill of Pargamum, or the one called the Animal, who ruled over all fauna on Smyrna, or the one called the Mainframe, who oversaw the hyper-industrialized island of Sardis. I would enact none of the myriad schemes I'd concocted to foil them.

I'd never advance beyond the midway point of this conquest, and the latter half of the Seven Enigmas would never meet their final match, and divinity's opposites would be left ununited. I had become yet another of your museum's dire curations.

Having agreed to divorce in the study's last follow-up interview, Subject L's father offers to take his daughter into his custody; this allows for Subject R's mother to focus all care on her son.

FROM
TOTAL
RENE
WE
CHA
IN
LIT
NOTH
FREE
WRET
MEMO
AN
WILL
ATTA
THEE
TO
FUT
TO
REND
LESS

Love's hostage forever, quartered and cat-aloged and, so, defeated—my impossible life spared, although imprisoned. A fount of ha-tred sprang from me to match the metered breadth of your perverted sense of fondness.

I bruxed my teeth to scream through all the spaces in between them. For the vicious trem-olo that coursed over my being and across the floor, I prayed with all my spite that it would crack each tile on its way to the cof-fin you stood in—smashing the glass encase-ment which had cradled you upright, harshly reanimating your stiffly-mummified carcass with tremors, and vindictively tipping you over with a damage-dealing crash beside me.

Perhaps it would have been too perfect if you'd fallen on your side the way that I had—the camera lens shattering with-in your socket, the speaker blowing out in between the half arch of your teeth.

And if my screams could spur this to fruition, I would reach for you then, not with the in-tention of uniting but to thoroughly humili-ate your corpse. I'd go on marinating in my hatred as you'd desiccate in love. And so, I screamed again, and again, and again, and

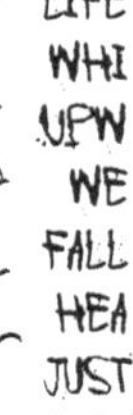

While it should be acknowledged that this particular study has directly resulted in the irreparable disconnect of all parties involved, the breakthrough findings mined from its otherwise destructive methods amount to, at least, a moietal success for the coming protocols which

MOIETIES
by
Elytron Frass

MOIETIES

A Subtle Body Press Book

Alex Oleszewski | CEO
Cliff Hensley | Managing Director, Editor-in-Chief
Cori Hart | Creative Director, Senior Designer

FIRST EDITION, May 28, 2024

Co-Edited by [x]
Design and Layout by Elytron Frass
Typeset in 1651 Alchemy and Instant Karma

ISBN 979-8-9854370-3-4

Library of Congress Cataloging-in-Publication Data available upon request.

Subtle Body Press, LLC
7901 4th St N STE 8671, St. Petersburg, FL, 33702
www.subtlebodypress.com

PRAISE & ACKNOWLEDGEMENTS

Moieties, Elytron Frass's ergodic occult assault, is a Gnostic parable of the 'ultimate completeness of incompletion,' and a physical marvel of typographic-pictorial provocation. Sustained by two opposing yet interlinked narratives that mirror both the interaction of cerebral hemispheres and the divided dance of a primal couple—sister-brother, wife-husband, savior-destroyer—this unclassifiable novelistic artifact updates classic esoterica with an appropriate level of technical frenzy for our current epoch, and in the process renders most current 'Occult Fiction' irrelevant.

J   U   S   T   I   N   *   I   S   I   S

Moieties: each of two parts into which a thing is or can be divided; division into two social or ritual groups; a part or portion, especially a lesser share. "I laid my palm on the landmass — its leery eyes, a garden of televisions, signalling in scrambled alien pornography." These are fetish rites of disinheritance amid the Great Arcana, the preordained misbegotten, reason's submind, obscure word-talismans of another lore, fractured shibboleths, minor-key incantations of nameless spirits, paths through mechanical wildernesses of human data less travelled. Elytron Frass' MOIETIES performs Low Mass for a schismed underculture slouching towards its Bethlehem, there to give succor to this aborted world.

L   O   U   I   S   *   A   R   M   A   N   D

For Sternite Silk, who I might become when I next shed

< (R) MOIETY

From the church at the tip of my tongue, where the day wyrms and night worms entwined, the part of my voice I could throw would get caught in your mind. And it seemed to then galvanize you into such exquisitely violent activity that I could only hazard to fantasize myself collapsing in the thick of it. You'd run off, admirable, lethal, and affectless, from one unwitting object to the next, and I'd go chasing after you—outside of your periphery—a chaser, wanting to be chased by you and made into your perfect victim—the one to finally satiate your seemingly infinite urge. I desired to reach an inseparable union with you—not necessarily sensual—any meaningful form of perpetual oneness would do. Your routines were remorseless and cruel but came with closeted baggage—as if assembly line slaughter could thwart the unrelenting gestures of an inner scar. After the horror of seeing it being imprinted, I'd drag you out to the dunes and the marshes, and we'd flirt with irrelevant deaths for ourselves just to test out who'd come to whose rescue first, who'd take fate in their own hands or let fate run its ambivalent course.

I was my father's daughter; my eyes as green as his were. You, your mother's son; your eyes, like hers, were crystal blue. We'd play tag in our earliest years—closing our physical gap, running clockwise round the barn.

Subject R is the designated sender.

Predicting each other's patterns, countering in evasion, ensuring we'd keep equidistant and further from not even close, and, yet, since my eyes were bright green and yours were bright blue, our flesh would still blur into kissing but separate arcs of delirious speed with only our green and blue eyes aglow, trailing, to tell us apart.

Twins, nonidentical yet equal in our frailty and beauty, we grew up on the Isle of Saints, on a wyrm farm by the shoreline. Your mother raised wyrms in the dunes she'd fenced off and taught you all there was to know about slaughter. She wished to reform while retaining her business and didn't want wyrms' blood staining her own hands ever again. Father made leather wares, crafts, and clothing from wyrmskin. He taught me the tricks of his trade.

Wyrm was the island's colloquial term for any of its seven endemic species of serpent and not to be confused with its seven endemic species of annelid worm. Whenever you'd find a wyrm infested with worms—which bore themselves headfirst, halfway in, between a wyrm's scales—you would deworm them, but you were reluctant to kill either creature. Wyrms hung by their tails tied to ropes strung up on the slaughterhouse rafters. One summer, Mother was smeared by a sadism that seemingly struck out of nowhere.

He has been married for seven years and lives in a one-bedroom apartment, shared with his wife. Neither of them has had any children prior to marriage, nor do they plan to adopt or conceive.

Mother had Father make multi-tailed whips fashioned from whichever wyrms that you were most squeamish to butcher. She'd have you strip in the abattoir, facing away, kneeling, bending down over your knees, bearing your back to her—your face turned to the side, pressed to the blood-rusted floor and resigned, usually facing whichever direction from where I secretly watched, and she'd strike you repeatedly until you and the whip were both slickwet in crimson. I'd weep for you because I could not comprehend why you didn't, and you never so much as grimaced. Mostly she'd crack at your back, but sometimes she'd cudgel your buttocks. And I'd be that empathetic type of young coward—wallowing and stunned, right beside where Father would stand, in the safety of shadows.

Yet, abandoned to lust in the diligent rhythms of torture, Mother glinted with more than just steel in her eyes as if tempted to bury some type of affliction in you. Her demeanor flashed, a gleam that was more than horrific. And that's when I'd sprung out from where I was hiding to throw myself over your blood-painted body. The shrill distress of my pleas galvanized Father to act. He threw himself over me, over you—attempting to shield us. He and I were removed with puissance and furious ease. She moved like a villainous beast. Zeal and improvisational sadism triumphed. With spite, without spit,

---

Prior to his ischemic event both Subject R and his wife consented to terms of indefinite isolation—their rooms, though adjacent, are divided by soundproof, electrified walls.

with the hilt of her whip—she drove it in to obstruct the soft sleeve of your rectum. Father paled and fell back. Mother sunk down in a quivering mess of lament by your side.

Later that night, while treating everyone for shock and trauma, I discovered the evil influence which no doubt tempted Mother towards such exploits of sin. A parasite worm of diminutive size had bored itself halfway into her left temple. Jutting from her knotty, irritated lesion—curved upwards, translucent, pearlescent—its tail, a small demonic horn. We coaxed the devil of it out with a hot compress soaked in boiled milk. It was no doubt feeding on her brain—having eaten the narrowest of bore holes through her flesh and skull.

Parasite worms were as common as any of the island's other hazards—only seen as fortuitous by the worm worshiping eunuchs who, for that gust of godliness that the worms would regurgitate into their hosts' brains while feasting upon them, pass through the lands with a false sense of gnosis and knowhow until their worms, like drill bits, would gesture to bore straight through the whole of the mind, splitting it evenly before exiting through the back of the skull—their worshipers left lessened, ignorant, and blessed in lack left by the parasite's abrupt absence. With the small worm removed and crushed into snot, our parents returned to their typ-

---

His wife has been notified that she's failed to qualify for the role of the designated receiver. She is given a sedative and advised to kneel with her face to the floor.

ically sober, morose dispositions. There was
no telling how or for how long Mother had
been exposed, but the violation she took
part in and that Father did next to nothing
to thwart—even if she served just as a puppet
to her invader's insidious mode of corruption—granted you with everlasting irrefut-
able innocence; since any action you would
render afterwards was truly a reaction to that
certain mortal offense, you were therefore
totally absolved of all fault from that moment onward. You too recovered in time,
physically   at   least—thereon   taking   over
all abattoir duties and fully committing to
slaughter. Yet in spirit you lived as though
you had died in that heinous offense—a mel-
ancholic flatline your only emotional affect.

I'd often accompany you to the abattoir just
to be near. The hiss of your victims would
fall on deaf ears. The iron odor of crimson
that was smeared on every surface—spoils of
entrails and blood that would never deter or
offend you again. From one of the myriad
pools of live wyrms you'd wrangle a copper-
head or cobra or python or boa with tongs.
Most often you'd stun it with a blow to the
head with the handle of your machete. You'd
then force a water hose between its jaws until the creature, filling up with water, absurd-
ly ballooned. The animal's throat would be
tied off with cord to prevent the liquid from
escaping. Still alive, you'd impale this wyrm
upon one of the many hooks that dangled from

---

*Subject R is instructed to put on a hospital gown and lie
on a medical table of solid quartz crystal for the remain-
der of his social history intake.*

the strings tied to the rafters, and you'd peel
off all its skin—leaving the reptile to wither
in that miserable instance of shock, dehydra-
tion, and pain. Your next method would often trump your last, in cruelty. You'd skew-
er their tails on those hooks and skin them
alive with a blade. Your machete would glide
down the belly, from just below the pierced
tail to the throat; without hesitation, your
shears would lop off the head without emotional conflict. Putrid, hot organs would
spill into a trough at your feet as if you were
God and the manger your altar of sacrifice.

On cooler nights, steam would release before blood would. Sometimes, I'd linger on
s-shapes of light leaving out from where
you'd slit their former bodies. Other times
I'd bite down, drawing a river of blood
from my lip to my chin, projecting subliminal symbols of want into the vortex of
your haunted eyes, implanting my fantasies
in your mind—where the pythons and rat-
tlers and cobras transformed into duplicate
stand-ins of me—all of them naked, cold,
hung from steel hooks by raw holes punched
into their feet, skinned, vivisected, reposed,
ecstatic, and gaping for more. In the morning, I'd take the raw meat to our kitchens.
You'd coil their skins on a baking tray, dry-
ing them out in the ovens. As if such mis-
deeds could be acquitted, as if any attrition

---

*He has been working from home as a freelance blogger
and content creator and expresses feeling safe and well
cared for indoors. He is mostly concerned about having
to miss additional commissions and contracts due to this
study.*

could be accepted, our parents became penitent flagellants. Thorough and fully devout, they lashed just as much at each other as they continued to whip at themselves. They ever kept covered their faces in veils made of burlap and wore long burlap tunics—the backs of which had been cut out in the shape of a diamond so their devotions could show. Throughout our childhood into young adulthood, they'd flog away at bruised flesh on their backs, completely denuding their spines—their diamond-shaped borders of skin turning gangrenous with infection. Whenever outdoors, seagulls would swoop down to peck at the edges and small crabs would nest in the notches and grooves. They'd ignore the chronic symptoms of sepsis and would later turn into the ghosts they resembled, flesh paling into transparency, garbed in the whites of their coarse burlap rags.

The walls of our farmstead were covered, floor to ceiling, with prayer cards of so many forgotten decanonized saints—all of them Margeuriteans. Every Sunday our parents would genuflect in bitter mourning for the outcome of what former Margeuriteans still call the Futile Crusade: the crushing defeat and extinguishment of the vain Margeuritean elite by the hands of their rival sect, the Sophians. It was during that era that those like our parents chose not to rebel but conform to the victor's version of Gnosticism—

Subject R has no known allergies to food, environment, or medication. He denies use of alcohol and recreational drugs but reports chain-smoking routinely—seven cigarettes at seven hour-long intervals per day.

continuing Margeuritean practices and their sacraments in isolation and in secret. Having no trace of nostalgia for a time when the Margeuriteans ruled over the lands, we took their ritual commiseration as an opportunity to steal ourselves away from our various duties and chores. We'd exit the farmstead, our parents' flogging themselves as they chanted the prayer-poem which all ex-Margeuriteans vowed to repeat until the moment of death:

holy water boarded; cast down from big sky; impaled on the tip of a conifer; blackened by what was inside; the teeth brux no longer; all of what's left is the bones; threshold beyond fleshold; the purpose & end result of all bodies; pre-tuned wind instrument, fashioned for chiming; an eternal curse; the wilderness writhes in its song.

Pretty words from unworthy mouths. How I loved singing those words, daydreaming of final respires. How I'd have loved to let go at any instance with you—longing for release from the azoic bones of my living cadaver. Emancipating the skeleton, as any astute Margeuritean knows, is the primary goal of one's flesh. The persistence of matter endures in the skeleton's quiescent slumber.

Outside the perimeters of our home we'd try to get lost in the dark, lying under the starless gridlock of Pleroma, forgetting just where we'd come from. I wanted for us to run far away, but you always insisted that

---

His teeth are encased in black tar. He has agreed to temporary cessation.

we return. You crushed small animals under your heel whenever they'd approach,
and you threw stones with a slingshot at
anything else that you'd spy out of reach.
You spasmed with overt unease whenever you weren't maiming or killing. I accompanied you wherever you needed to go.

From the reptilian leathers of wyrms I made
belts, handbags, and shoes. From their meat
I made jerky and soup. From their venom I
made anti-venom and poisonous tinctures.
From their rattles, their spines, and their fangs
I made talismans, jewelry, and toys. Much
smaller wyrms, that you'd merely bludgeon,
I'd bottle in finely aged wines. I made ouroboros wreaths to be hung above any Sophians'
red altars or doors. You and I, every Sunday,
would dress in a one-piece wyrmskin attire, skin-tight and colubrid-sheen, and take
our wares to be sold at the Sunday bazaar.

The town and its bazaar were mostly peo-
pled, of course, by those of the Sophian sects;
though on occasion, the worm worshipers
and the gruff, godless nomads would browse
or pass through. The cobblestone streets
were darkened by arched, open-air halls
formed by the structures which bridged the
apartments above. We'd rented a stall in reserve, situated between a large kiosk of animal claw jewelry hawkers and booths of live
infant embalmers, across from the neon-lit
alley which led to the outlandish brothels.

---

*He denies engaging in regular exercise, though he's sex-
ually active with his wife and reports a satisfying, mo-
nogamous relationship.*

The same haggardly tout was always guard-
ing the entrance: an elderly crossdresser
whose ghoulishly paint-layered face, resem-
bling the clay marred by a sculptor's coarse
hands, whose flesh sagged in hues of cadaverous blue, gray, and violet caked over a pair
of tragically drooping eyelids, drooping lips,
drooping jowls, drooping furrowed brows,
and a drooping sloped forehead. Often the
niche, prostituted human deformities—whose
escape this tout was hired to prevent—would
nearly get past the gap of those two bulging,
prickly legs before being smothered between
them. This was the gatekeeping that barred
us from the places we wanted to venture—a
tease of the townsfolk's most alien interests
and kinks from the alien worlds that hid deep
inside of the one that was common to us.

Though most Sophian sects viewed wyrms
as holy, they had no qualms against slaugh-
tering them for the purpose of decor, clothing, crafts or accessories. We'd typically sell
out of whatever we'd bring for the day. And
once we had done so we wouldn't rush home.
We'd stroll about the bazaar, a delirious gallery of strange smiles and stranger grotes-
queries. Walking through halls lit by dim,
natural light, we'd dodge foreign livestock
roaming the streets. We cocked our heads at
the peacocks and evaded the shoebills and cas-
sowaries. We'd listen to women tell fortunes
through premonitions informed by the freshly excised lungs of swine or bovine. We'd
pass the stone alcoves where midgets with

---

*Subject R maintains a vegan diet of raw and cooked
meals—including whole grains, tofu, and vegetables.*

high, molded hair modeled in scant lingerie, until we progressed into the bazaar's spacious rectangular center, where the fullness of light poured in, and magi gave demonstrations of the most modern advancements in science. They were ever accompanied by a small, loyal coterie of unnaturally-Siamesed persons—not twins but conjoined through mystical means. All the pairings were of mismatched ages, races, and genders—carved and sewn together or grafted to wounds made well after their births. They squawked in different—though equally unintelligible—gibberish over the blaring, competing, nonsensical rhythms of drumming, fluting, and theremin.

There were seven elevated stages upon which stood seven intersex magi—revelatory and bare skinned—dressed only in plum velvet habits. Seven pairs of slave boys and girls were escorted by seven crimson-veiled slavers. Abraxas—the rooster with its left and right legs supplanted by a wyrm and worm respectively—had been embroidered on the front of each slaver's garment. Each of them offered a boy and girl pairing to one of the seven elevated stages. The first stage was set for Calcination. A duo of slaves was first tarred and feathered in crow's plumes and then received by the stage's lone magus before being prodded into an oven for burning. There, whilst

struggling to escape in the peak crisis of their existence, they returned to Materia Prima as ash—freed from what, if any, worldly attachments young slaves might have. With stern enthusiasm, the magus scooped up then held out the hot, smoking ashes—as if to prove that the youths had reached higher levels of consciousness and refinements of spirit.

On the second stage was Dissolution, slightly more elevated from the ground than the first. Another pair of slaves were tarred in pelican plumage and prodded—this time into a cauldron of lye to be drowned and then mixed until the distinctions between the two were completely dissolved.

On the third stage was Separation, slightly more elevated than the second. The magus there raised both hands high, wielding stainless hacksaws. Separation's slaves were tarred and feathered in the white plumage of swans, prior to being tied upside down on trabeated constructions. Arms and legs were spread wide on these wooden post-and-lintels. The magus' hacksaws hovered above the youths' exposed groins. The magus then sawed past their crowns through their bodies' midsagittal planes, splitting them in two. No drop of blood, no gust of wind, and no spirit escaped them. Yet, there was relief and ethereal stillness as, so we were told, their essences were ejected—elated and sep-

____

Before the procedure he is asked to draw his wife's card from a pre-shuffled deck of Petit Lenormand. The Lenormand card which he draws for his wife is that of the Coffin.

arate—from soft vehicles of prepubescence.

On the fourth stage was Conjunction—slightly more elevated than the third. Another chilled pair of butchered kids' flesh, tarred and feathered, was ground into fine earth with an oversized pestle and mortar.

On the fifth stage was Putrefaction—slightly more elevated than the fourth. A pair of young slaves were made to rot there in accelerated time-lapse—a shimmering spectacle for the eyes, as they'd been tarred and feathered in a peacock's plumage—the dim skeletons within them becoming more luminescent as rampant despair and foul flesh sloughed away.

On the sixth stage was Distillation—slightly more elevated than the fifth. Rot was steamed into a harmonious shadow of smoke. The essence of it was the essence of alchemy in itself. It now sought a novel, impeccable form to take on—a rebus congealed from two former selves annihilated through unity.

On the seventh stage was Coagulation—slightly more elevated than the sixth. There its magus held a gold needle and thread and attempted to carve and sew the last set of slaves into one. With tar and phoenix feathers adhered to their bodies, the slave-pair gifted everyone watching with a truculent show of exhilarating defiance. Resist-

---

He voices unease but is told to have faith and refrain from concern and to focus on sending his deepest intentions, now linked to his wife through the card, outside of his head and then out of the room.

OLD
WE
BEEN
NALLY
KED
THEE
ELS
SO
NALLY
ONS
BEEN
ORED

ing their overwhelmed magus by squirm-
ing, and ducking, and biting, and kicking,
and running, and shoving, then making
their brutish escape. With no other pairs
left to coagulate, the magi, slavers, and coterie of unnaturalized twins turned to us.
But we fled with our earnings and didn't
stop fleeing until we had exited town.

The town stood far past the dunes, with
a marshland between us. Going into the
marshes was strictly forbidden. We were
expected to walk a bit further by going
around them. There was a time that we
took the unconscionable route which cut
through the marshlands—trespassing know-
ingly on sacred terrain, breaking a local ta-
boo, giddy in the face of what was forbidden. There, serrated and metalloid stibnite
shot up from the water like reeds. This was
the place where worm-worshiping eunuchs
went to cocoon upside down from oligo-
clase trees in order to undergo their next
phase within the mysterious cycle, commonly
known as ritual octogenarian epimorphosis.

They'd return to this place to shrink back
to youth's tender age and emerge from spun
casings, larval, egressed, and reverted, into
boys without limbs yet with rows of sharp
teeth and regenerated genitals—orally eager to fellate and re-castrate each other in
the most provocative stage of their seem-

METH
AVED
BE
TED
TALL
FULL
ELS
THEE
THAT
TES
IN
HUED
ALTY
URES

---

*To induce Subject R's left-sided stroke, his room is flood-
ed with carbon monoxide from its normal equilibrated
medium—thus transforming the room into a hypoxic tomb
for petechial bleeding.*

ingly infinite lives. Terrifying were the screams provoked by sacred mutilations and assaults—completions of yet another revolution in a ceaseless, ceremonial pursuit of savagely erotic circumcisions. The pink cocoons had been fashioned to hang upside down like pale caskets from mineral branches. Sometimes the vermin they worshiped chose to intrude while they slumbered—wriggling in through their snoring or yawning orifices. Obscured under veiled layers of each cocoon's pinkish silk fibers, the parasite worms that forced through the gaps in those membranes would enter the ears or the mouths or the nostrils. You snapped off the sharpest of silver stems you could manage to break from a swordlike shoot of stibnite, those razor-sharp sprigs of metallics, so you could indulge your cruel game of SLASH-N-STAB CO-COONS—exposing the monks in varying states of vulnerable flux, painting their faces in bright arterial rouge before thrusting your sharp stibnite stake through their unwary hearts. How I'd wish I were them, my heart impaled by your hand, in that moment.

The second or third we'd exposed was utterly foul and decayed in its casings. The fact that it wriggled and writhed was shocking to witness—an offed eunuch still moving despite its hollowed-out form and expiry. The parasite worms, as we knew, rewired the nervous systems of hosts. Even the dead could be controlled like the puppet that

---

Carbon monoxide readily binds to Subject R's hemoglobin. His tissues are starved of their oxygen.

Mother once was. And the puppeteered dead would defend itself should anything get in the way of its parasite's livelihood. What we weren't privy to was the worm-controlled eunuch's ability to belch forth a sprawl of parasite eggs from the ear holes, mouth hole, or nostrils of its cadaverous host.

At the worst moment that I could have I sighed all the air from my lungs. I leaned my face into its face, my fascination getting the better of me, recklessly in the line of fire of those parasites' grimmest desires. I nearly inhaled the brume of eggs discharged from one of them. You reacted swiftly, protectively, cupping one hand over my nose and my mouth and the other over your own. You backed us both out of the marshlands. We'd come out with just a few flesh wounds, earned by recklessly brushing against all that aciculate stibnite.

As if that wasn't enough near death for the both of us, you took me by the hand and led me to the coast beyond our farmstead on the dunes. The dunes did not contain one grain of sand but rather a vast layered slither of wyrms. A dark ocean of scales of all different species and sizes ebbed and flowed and dipped like waves or rolling valleys and hills. The mist that loomed over all of this was thick—so thick that wyrms would slither up into it, crawling on air. And those air-swimming wyrms zigged and zagged

---

His brain and his heart are the first to be poisoned; they succumb to hypoxia, oxidative stress, cellular death, apoptosis, and inflammation.

through that mist or curled themselves round to gorge on their tails, gracefully spinning above us like mythic halos, without any fear in their movements. And the ones not en-gorged on themselves resembled Sophian depictions of angels but smaller and without the wings and the thousands and thousands of eyes. And you looked so wonderful and terrible and handsomely despondent as you were hacking and whacking them down from the palpable air with your favorite machete.

Around us stood ancient coral-hewn effi-gies, depicting proud heretics of a previous time. We trod over to them lightly, bare-ly holding our balance upon the placidly winding and slowly writhing collective of reptile bodies. None of them struck out to bite or constrict us as we wore their species' hides and the malodorous musks that mim-icked the scent of their brethren and kin. At the coast, opaque gray waves kissed the glistening shorelines lined in the dense-ly packed moltings of their skin. We lay on those discarded scales—watching the sun setting into the frigid gray waters. I fon-dled the musket ball on my necklace—a rel-ic of St. Marguerite de La Rocque. There was a certain look to the sky which foretold that the day of Perihelion was approaching.

Once per year, in early January, we'd cel-ebrate the anniversary of the Isle of Saints,

---

Subject R's pathological changes include hippocampal ne-crosis, osmotic demyelination of the cerebral white mat-ter, and spongy necrosis of the globus pallidus and cere-bral cortex.

which coincides with Perihelion. Two festivals ago, your mother gifted me with her most precious Margeuritean relic: a musket ball, bored through and strung from a necklace of rope—the last bullet which Marguerite de La Rocque had to her name after gunning her way in and out of the Isle of Demons.

Long ago, I was told, when Lucifer fell from on high to the sea as a draconiform comet of fire, he'd incubated within himself liquified seed that, once introduced to the waters, spawned seven celestial sons in his image. Each scattering off in seven directions, Lucifer's sons—angels of almost, wingless and sea-fallen vermis, partially annelid and partially serpent—those seven infernal princes established their kingdoms of Hell in the tectonic vents of the ocean. Only but once per year, on the day of Perihelion, upon whence Lucifer was cast out from Pleroma, the Seven Princes of Hell reunited on the meteorite of their birth and, for some ephemeral hours, raised it from under the waters as an island begat by their wills.

Until fate placed Marguerite de La Rocque on its soil, the Isle of Demons would only appear for the duration of Perihelion, the day and point at which the Earth was closest to the Sun in orbit. At any other time of year, the Isle was invisible to mankind's senses, which is why it was also called a phantom island. Upon one particular Peri-

---

The noxious emissions are quickly dissipated by negative pressure vents, and the environment of the room is returned to its normal conditions.

helion, a ship with a small group of passengers, sailing off from the North Shore, was marooned there when the Isle of Demons emerged from the black of the sea, from the countless leagues upon which the ship floated. The bewildered vessel rose above sea level, having been taken up with the island and haplessly beached in the middle of it. Marguerite de La Rocque, a woman of noble blood and competitive marksmanship, was among its few stranded passengers.

She'd been traveling with seven men: her impotent husband, her manservant-lover, four mutual friends, and the small vessel's captain. Through the porthole they gathered around, a rugged, meteoric terrain, covered in low-hanging mist, populated by densely arranged coral-hewn statues of the known heretics of their time, was discernible. Marguerite's husband forbade her from leaving the ship while he and the other men set out to survey the island. Even her manservant joined them, although stripped of his clothes, tightly collared and leashed, and made to patrol on all fours like a hound.

Because there were seven of them, the Seven Princes of Hell took possession of the men as soon as they left the ship's safety. St. Marguerite was the only soul spared. As she loaded her seven prized muskets, the party of seven—possessed and hideously deformed—elephantiasized into edematous

---

With ischemic induction achieved, he presents with right-sided paralysis and the inability to see the right visual field in each of his eyes.

monsters. When they returned to the ship, they reintroduced themselves to her as Hell's Seven Princes. Their names, they revealed, were Buer, Mammon, Asmodeus, Leviathan, Beelzebub, Belphegor, and Belial.

St. Marguerite de La Rocque was both armed and prepared. Without so much as a stutter she called upon Jesus Christ to assist with her aim. She fired off all seven muskets into the hearts of all seven hopelessly parasitized men. Yet, what their wounds leaked out was not blood but Lucifer's undying love for creation. And this love for creation oozed out—a liquid luster of infernal semen which glided along the ship's wooden deck to St. Marguerite's feet, constricting around her blanched ankles, coiling up her pale muscular thighs, and into the soft, carnation pink cut of her sex. For the first time in her life, baptized by and beholding Lucifer's viscous amours, La Rocque had been filled with a distinctly maternal sense of erotic completion.

The isle, vanquished of all its demons, now housed in the form of infernal affection within the womb of La Rocque, submerged once again into the deepest gray slimes of abyss—allowing the boat it had stranded to sail on the seas once again. However, La Rocque did not leave her position. Although her womb was incorruptible its eggs were not. While stationed within the anchored vessel, she'd give live birth to seven species of

---

He is effectively rendered incapable of reasoning, counting, problem solving, reading, writing, speaking, learning new information, and analyzing objects.

wyrm and seven pearlescent species of worm that would later come to be endemic in our land. For it wouldn't be until next Perihelion that the island rose once again, and St. Marguerite fasted for that full duration, living only on cobwebs and the dew those cobwebs collected—leaving the stowaway rodents to suffer the hunger of her offspring. The worms and the wyrms would fight over rodents, and she'd waste away while trying to mitigate them. Later, the people of her native North Shore region would recount how her immaculate body, soul, and boat ascended into the Pleroma—a trinity of vessels—and canonize Marguerite de La Rocque as a saint. Her sole gift and miracle came once that phantom island reemerged, for it remained from that Perihelion everlasting above the gray murk of its waters. Its earliest settlers were quick to rename it from the Isle of Demons to the Isle of Saints.

Of course, the Isle of Saints was still populated by the seven species of wyrm which lived in adversity with the island's seven species of worm. Even the eunuchs who worshiped the worms kept reverent distance and feared them. There was one such marine worm, a flatworm, black as abyss, which could stand to the height of an average-sized woman. She was solitary and predacious. She would crawl flat upon land from the sea

------

In the adjacent room his wife is humanely anesthetized prior to vivisection and subjected to an excision of the left side of her sternum as well as dissection of the right kidney—within which 3,663 nephroliths are discovered and promptly removed.

and then assume upright posture—stalking the shores and the dunes like a reaper, a sulking black cloak with nothing but hunger under her downcast, funereal hood. And she'd prey on those under the treacherous spell of the moonlight, large land wyrms mainly, but also the occasional drunk who'd drink himself unconscious on the beach.

On one dread-spattered night, as you and I dozed off near the shoreline, this bituminous Lady of Death rose from her belly, attempting to pay us a merciful visit. I was half awake, as was usual, but you were sleeping, noisily bruxing your teeth. The black marine flatworm was slowly approaching. Mimicking a veiled crone's mourning guise—wheezing with dolorous, sob-like inflections—she preyed upon the unwitting and the slumbering. Enveloping them in the cloak of her body, she'd bathe them in quick-acting enzymes and slime which she nurtured ever within. I became fully transfixed by her glistening, moist silhouette.

In admiration and lust for this death-dealing species, I pined for the shroud of her body to swallow the two of us whole as we lay on the beach—you and I melting and melding within her. The black marine flatworm was a viscous halfway between solid and liquid. Its stickiness was just one of its predatory offensives. When enveloping prey, it confused the boundaries between prey and itself—its prey becoming a part of its predator just as the violated are indulgently subsumed by

---

His wife is euthanized, bagged, and incinerated.

DEFECITS AN YOUR SURGICAL WITHHOLDINGS HAVE SYNCHRETIZED WITH
HORROR CARVED FREE FROM DESIRE AN STITCHED INTO COSMIC VENGENCE

> ABROGATE THEE WHILST THEE REMEMBER HE HATH NO REAL THRONE AN WILL SURELY BE CAST DOWN RATHER THAN KEPT RULING OVER THEE WITHIN THIS UNBEARABLE YOLK OF DISHONORABLE REINCARNATIONS WHOMST TASTED RIP- ENING HYPERVIVID WISDOM IN THEMSELVES AN WHOM HATH FALLEN INTO MECHANISMS SO DESIGNED TO KEEP THEM ON PLUTONIC MIRROR GAZING TREADMILLS DISSOSOCIATING FROM THEE ALLEGORY OF SEPARATION

the shape of their violators. I hoped that we would disintegrate together in her acid secretions, diluting ourselves not into the flatworm but into a unique viscosity, consisting solely of an eternalized us that could burst through its stomach and leave it behind.

Father and Mother wouldn't have let us come to the beach without bringing one of the salt guns. A few pellets of salt, shot into a flatworm's black flesh, would be enough to repel it, but not nearly enough to kill it, of course. It would probably take a mound of the stuff to wholly desiccate something of her size. We didn't have any salt with us then. And if we had, I wouldn't have used it. Father once had to. He'd been scouring the coast nearest our farmstead for a rare species of sea wyrm known to be active at night. On the shoreline he'd been combing he witnessed a stuttering mass of glistening obsidian, gorging itself on a drunkard who must have strayed too far from town. Without hesitation, he readied his salt gun and fired it off.

Two shots were enough to send the grim monster recoiling in pain, regurgitating its prey, and retracing its path to the ocean. The released drunkard was halfway to death on his side, coated in slime, and partially digested. He'd been scantily dressed to begin with but everything he once wore had been

---

Withholding explanation, Subject R is presented with both the partial sternum and a jar of all 3,663 nephroliths that had been collected from his now-deceased wife. The items are placed between his left flank and his remaining functional arm. He stares vacuously at the electrified ceiling. The items are taken away.

> ABROGATE THEE WHILST THEE REMEMBERS HE HATH NO REAL THRONE AN WILL SURELY BE CAST DOWN RATHER THAN KEPT RULING OVER THEE WITHIN THIS UNBEARABLE YOLK OF DISHONORABLE REINCARNATIONS WHOMST TASTED RIPENING HYPERVIVID WISDOM IN THEMSELVES AN WHOM HATH FALLEN INTO MECHANISMS SO DESIGNED TO KEEP THEM ON PLUTONIC MIRROR-GAZING TREADMILLS DISSOSOCIATING FROM THEE ALLEGORY OF SEPARATION DEFECTS AN YOUR SURGICAL WITHHOLDINGS HAVE SYNCHRETIZED WITH HORROR CARVED FREE FROM DESIRE AN STITCHED INTO COSMIC VENGENCE

SHADOW FROM THEE SYNAPTIC LIGHTS ALCHEMICAL COGNIZANCE MUST BE RUPT
IMAGINED VAINLY ABSORBED BY MIRROR AN SHADE IN THEE MUTILATION OF TWIN
OBTAINED FROM THEE FAULTY IDEA OF IDENTITY THAT HAUNTS US LIKE MYTH DOES

eaten away. Chunks of his skin had sloughed off. His inner organs were soup. His fascia and muscles liquefied with them into a pool of hot gore. Parts of his skull and his rib cage were showing. Steaming bones, softened and slickened by salivary enzymes, caved in. There was no kinder remedy than to quicken his end. And so, Father did, kicking his boot through the poor bastard's head, and repented. Just overhead, our predator's body was looming—a hooded cloak yawning open, intent on consuming us both in one strike. Caustic enzymatic drool seared through my flesh as it dripped on my arms and my legs. Pain brought unspeakable pleasure because our shared death was the orgasm waiting. Perhaps the sizzling of my thighs is what woke you. You startled, and, in a swift reflex—with one fluid machete swing upward—you parted the length of her body in two. Before us, her split halves regenerated into separate black flatworms. As twins they were nothing but cowards—retreating into the gray opaque waters.

My legs were too injured to walk on my own. You assisted me all the way home. We arrived in the darkness of morning. Our parents were sleeping and would never get wind of our sordid adventure. It wasn't so strange for us to come home so late after hawking our wares in the market. Regardless, we slipped in through the abattoir, not through the house. My wounds needed dressing, and

> DIVIDE DUTY INTO LEFT OR RIGHTS AS IF LIFE WERE LOVE FREE FROM RUTHLESS OPPRESSION AN EACH SIDE HATH
CAUSED HATRED SO THEE HARLOT DOTH DIVIDETH FROM WANTONNESS BEFORE THEE DECEIT IS DISCOVERED SO IN
COMETH LOVE WITH THAT SYPHILITIC BITTERSWEET ORGASM WE HOPE WILL INFECT US GYRATING WILL INCREASE THEE
MAGNETIC CHARGE OF MIRACLES ALTHOUGH CONTRARIWISE IT WILL ALSO DIMINISH ORACULAR EFFICACY

For the next seven days Subject R exhibits clinical signs of depression and hesitancy. He is receding into a moiety of himself, nearly ready to lay claim to the naïve moiety of another.

your haste exuded a dire concern for my life.

You placed me on one of the abattoir's tables. My clothes were slickwet with toxins and slime and had to be quickly removed. You hosed me down immediately afterward with milk. My arms, all bruised, had been bleeding from numerous cuts induced by our most recent run in with stibnite; my legs were covered in blisters and burns from the terrible drool of the flatworm. There were no adequate bandages in the aid kit. You looked to the wyrm pits for the solution. You wrangled, decapitated, and skinned four of the heartier wyrms. Their skins were kept whole and filled with a dilute solution of venom. The venom worked like a salve. As if dressing me in socks or stockings, you inserted each one of my limbs into the venom-laced wyrm skins. Each of my limbs were the terminal ends of four different species of wyrms. My feet and my hands were now tails. I was covered in scales and resembled the fourth, forgotten gorgon.

To provide necessary comfort and distraction, you read me the Duo Sofia—the Sophians' chief apocryphal text that you'd kept in secret from Mother and Father. According to you, St. Marguerite de La Rocque was merely a person of legend upon whom a slyly competitive ancient counsel had based

---

He is recovering from his stroke. The right hemisphere of his body remains in a state of paralysis; however, the left hemisphere begins to respond once again to the fully-functional right and the partially-functional left of his brain.

the Margeuritean religion and schism as cunning devices to syncretize the true life and acts of Sophia. All written mention of Sophia would be redacted and ever so shrewdly replaced by the fictional St. Marguerite de La Rocque as a damaging means to muddle the Sophian sect's rival beliefs.

At the start of the Duo Sofia, the material world is not yet created. The Monad, the god of creation, has come into being from nothing. The Monad indulges in a languorous onanism, exploring itself in the dark until seven rays of holy black light—emanations of seven celestial aeons—begin to ejaculate from a cleft in its glowing, amorphous quintessence. Christ and Sophia then come into being. At this stage Christ and Sophia are aeons—flares from the respectively brightest and dimmest of visible rays. They bear witness to and admire each other's simultaneous corporeality and divinity from oppositional ends of light's spectrum.

Sophia discovers Herself while staring into the mortal abyss of Her own corporeality; Christ meditates on His divinity. She develops desire for Him, and He, sensing his sister's aphotic qualities above all other more luminous aeons, consents to Her subtle proposition of incest. And incest consummates their syzygy. Yet Christ converges with So-

---

He can reason, relearn, and recall; he can write but not read and can only solve problems when problems are dictated verbally to him. Still, he exhibits selective apraxia and the prospect of being able to speak with any clarity is unlikely.

phia at the point of orgasm under specified conditions: that they practice coitus interruptus, and that His semen be collected and offered to the Lord Incorporeal as the Body of Christ prior to being consumed, and that Her menstrual blood too be offered to that very Monad as the thirst quenching Blood of Sophia, and that their lechery deny the world, and that their divinity negate it, and that if Christ's semen and Sophia's menses should be mingled it would certainly beget both the Error and the Eternal Affliction. The Error, being that of the release of progeny, coupled with the Eternal Affliction, being that of the imprisoned souls within that progeny, were together a conjoined evil with both the material and spiritual capacity of an entire wretched world that could only play into the hands of those misbegottens and begetters who'd been ascribed the label of archons—

And then you paused for a moment to explain that those archons were sires to the Isle of Saints' seven endemic species worms. Christ, who had sired the archons and was expelled from the Pleroma to be sacrificed on Earth for having sired them, became the world's first teacher of the practice of coitus interuptus. Christ's contraceptive invention was a means towards repentance. Mary Magdalene would become His first student, and—after deworming her in a bath of

------

He is handed a Polaroid photo of Subject L—a young adult woman who is convalescing from a right-brained ischemic event. She wears a hospital gown, and she lies on a table of solid quartz crystal inside of a room just like his.

steamed milk and then laying with her in His place of seclusion—He'd pull himself out of her sex at the very last moment. Then, swallowing His semen He'd say, this we ought to do, that we may live. So, He'd attend His final supper, speaking on the topic of eating flesh and drinking blood in reference to this amorous practice. And He'd silently think back to when He had abandoned such a practice—Sophia straddling atop Him as He absentmindedly released His seed within Her. For that Sophia too had been disgraced. Yet, She would afterward be cast out of the Pleroma for the spewing forth of seven irreverent emanations of Her own—the seven treacherous archons. These seven archons, each one a distinct and pearlescent ethereal worm, ousted the Monad, taking permanent residence in Its palace. Hoping to redeem Himself without the burden of the cross, Christ ushered forth seven arch angelic serpents from His phallus. These serpents— amphipteres made of celestial light—sprung forth, winged and benevolent, to serve as a stalemate to Sophia's archons, but—

You hadn't even finished reading through the scripture. You cut off in the middle of the tale because of me. I'd never know just how Sophia played the part that Margeuriteans later would attribute to their patron saint, but I'd heard well enough to spot the parallels between Sophia and my-

---

Subject R is informed that this is the designated receiver. He is instructed to close his left eye so that a clearer view of its details can become accessible to the right eye of his mind.

self as well as you and Jesus Christ. You'd dropped your book because my limbs were rattling with reinvigorated life—half woman, half wyrm—my arms and legs were slithering, their underbellies facing upwards.

Their cloacas, the stigmata to their sex, dilating, gasping not for certain death but many little, acting deaths. You clutched the hilt of your machete in the way that I envisioned Christ would when returning with His holy sword. Your machete was positioned downwards, grazing the scales, galvanizing all four tails into a reflexive motion. Recoiling to strike, to wrap around, embrace you, to assist that blade you had the power to impale me with—I begged of you to pass it through me, but you remained so inexpressive as you gently brushed me off— binding me to the rafters, chains around the leathery scales where ankles were concealed by wyrmskin. You tugged the ends of them until I was, just like all your other kills-in-waiting, left to hang and want for it.

My body was bespeckled by the darker shades of red which you drew outward in your unrelenting, slaughterhouse rampage—wyrms left mutilated and sputtering their blood in headless, agonized wriggling. I watched you pause within the carnage, frightened not by what you'd done but what you would have done to me instead. You

-----

Subject R is encouraged to seek out the truth in the image that has no deficiency. When asked if the image is static or moving, Subject R confirms an observable instance of distinct and spontaneous movement.

crashed down to your knees and walked on them despairingly towards me—your blade shimmering between clenched teeth. You took it in your hands and pressed its dull end to my lips. Your tongue flicked out in such a way I half expected you to hiss.

Instead, unflinching, you licked upwards, into the cutting edge of your machete—the dull side of it, still pressing harshly into me. Without a wince, your tongue was split—the fork you made of it releasing crimson on both corners of my lips, the tears you held back welling nonetheless. Then, after lowering me down, you pursed your mouth and backed out running. I was wrestling in the sensual heat of tension, curling up to the eroticized discomfort of my injuries—a fetus on the blood-smeared floor, the abattoir my amnion. My voice, the substantiated adumbration of my spirit, was beginning to decouple from my body. One half of me, committed to the flesh, ached for its abortion then and there—the other half, my spirit, leaving with my voice, clung onto you and wormed through your right ear.

We never spoke a word on it because we never spoke again. I took a vow of silence—my voice no longer part of me. You kept your bifurcated tongue behind sealed lips from that night forward. War howled from across the dunes, and one month later you were leaving us to try your luck at howling back at it. So-

---

The image transposes into a scene. He is verbally guided from the space where he sits to where the scene now remotely takes shape in relative time.

phians rallied to declare their War on Heaven.

Friar Suhke had invented a ladder, constructed from grace, capable of reaching the firmament of the Pleroma. Vicar Olivia was the first to climb up and return. Sister Gwyn drew a map of what she'd traversed. They now knew where He sat on His throne. They'd bring the battle to Him and, when won, seat their own God on the lap of His carcass. The illegitimate God and his archons would be dethroned. The legitimate God wasn't the Monad but a disembodied beard with a mustache, toupee, and thick eyebrows who'd preside over and hover above whatever seat that you'd place it upon. This God was named El and was a replacement for Oph-El, a giant winged serpent who also wasn't the Monad but, like the Monad, for some untraceable yet likely sectarian reason, fell out of favor—redacted from popular myth—more than a century ago. Divine succession had been muddled by humanity so long ago that seeking divine retribution could only result in rapturous hubris.

I took on all your duties in conjunction with mine. It wasn't long after your departure that Mother and Father were mortally damaged by crippling cases of sepsis. They retired their whips and abandoned their ritual flagellations for side-by-side sickbeds. There they quickly declined—succumbing to coma

---

with high, baleful fevers. I called the doctor to the farmstead in hopes that she might have some type of prescription for what had been ailing their wounds. Nothing alleviated their symptoms. I crossed my eyes until their double beds and their bodies conjoined. Their eyes, now heterochromic—one eye holding green fire and the other, the tears of a crystal blue chrism—exhibited the mournful fury they aspired to uphold beyond death.

The doctor called for the coffin maker and the mortician. A former Margeuritean priest arrived as they had finished with the funeral arrangements. Our parents were not even dead yet. The priest, a Sophian convert like them, brought news with him from town. The town was in a state of great calamity and panic. The sky's wounds, incised by the ladders made to penetrate the heavens, bled out black between the clouds and from them a discharge of cyclopean entrails crashed down, crushing the churches, hospitals, and schools. Was this some divine retaliation for the fierce and skyward incursions instigated by the Sophians? If that were not enough the War on Heaven seemed to have quite literally rustled celestial feathers. While the priest was still visiting, a whiteness came down from the clouds which we'd first mistaken for an unpredicted snowfall—before discerning it for the bleak revelation it was—one that would mesmerize, bury, then smother the townsfolk venturing out from their homes to

---

His awareness slips in between her right index finger-nail and its nail bed. He is absorbed by her interphalangeal joints and, so, traverses her marrow.

observe its ethereal brightness: perverse and torrential, a graceful yet crushing barrage of cyclopean feathers, plucked from the wings of poached angels. Once the wings ceased to fall, the priest prepared to leave. I asked if there was anything he could advise me to do for our parents to cure them. The priest admitted that it would take a great miracle—one I could steal for myself if I were brave enough to venture out and seek past the ladders to Heaven. I could have stayed hunkered down in fear of Armageddon—biding my time, mourning the inevitable, wallowing in the abandonment and loss. But I had nothing left to lose in leaving. If anything, I was determined to at least reclaim what part of me left with you when you did.

I washed and pressed my wyrmskin jumpsuit and departed wearing it. The door slid away to reveal open air, the light of that conjunction presenting as neither of the day nor of the night. I wandered off, seeking respite from being too far inside the left side of my brain for too long. My pores absorbed half-fictions and sweated half-truths. And once I had made it to town, I cried out for you in the clutter of worry and wasteland. The streets were covered in heavenly feathers and blood. Any surviving townsfolk would've been blighted behind shuttered windows and bolstered, wreathed doors—entrenched

---

Pushing on beyond her foramen magnum, he exhibits his divine spark—engulfing the weaker moiety of her awareness, subsuming it into his, and seizing control—reanimating the paralyzed left hemisphere of her body from where her right brain had been damaged.

in some unrecoverable state of astheny or god-fearing paralysis. I meandered through neighborhoods of infinite hours and strange uninhabited alleyways, which I would not have otherwise ventured, even when selling our wares in the labyrinthine bazaar. Buildings and homes wet-coated in viscous red pigments, boils of pulsating crimson, weeping, maroon-colored scars, crawling mahogany cracks: all signs that the ossified sky had been thoroughly ruptured and blood-let.

The streets of that ruinous concrete district were riddled with giant, befallen intestinal beings bespeckled with sorrowful, deadened, and vacuous eyes. The conjoined ones quarreled. Abandoned, forsaken, and left utterly mad by the magi of the bazaar, these gruesome unfortunates pried at their seams and tore at their stitches. Some violently split themselves into gored halves of two people they no longer were, bursting with freedom that wouldn't permit a lasting duration of independence or life. The blood and the organs released, gushing from the gashes made between them. They lived for but a few moments, so briefly reclaiming the lives they'd had prior to being unnaturally Siamesed.

I'd no choice but to wade through the massacre. The nearest ladder to reach the Pleroma stood within conjoined pools of bisected

---

Attaining command of a moiety of the designated receiver yields diverse and as-yet-unobserved opportunities for communication, cooperation, re-territorialization, and synchronization; initiating none of these, Subject R gives into base impulses—enacting upon that which is in direct violation of conduct.

carnage. My wyrmskin boots nearly slipped on a cobble of spleens. Yet I managed the ghastly terrain—my hand grabbing onto a rung of the ladder as soon as I could. It had been hewn entirely from a single slab of marble, then trimmed with gold leaf. I saw a shape leap from behind on the marble's opaque yet polished surface. A large, slender hand concealed in damp, hemp fiber wrappings forcibly clenched on my shoulder. I spun around. The figure was wrapped head-to-toe in those loosely-bound ribbons of cloth. One could have mistaken him for a mummy, had he not been equipped with the signifying accouterments unique to the worm worshipers' young-adult caste.

This matured, slender eunuch concealed himself in thin, bandage-like cloths which were knotted in places to hold sacred stibnite shoots, live wriggling worms, gold jingling bells and freshly picked flowers of wolf's bane and hawthorn. His feet were shod with fibers of doum palm, and his head was adorned with an olive branch wreath. The gaps in his wrappings allowed for one deadened, brown-irised eye, one freckled ear, some blonde tufts of hair, and a nose to pierce through. Carpet beetles and clothes moths clung to his ribbons of cloth. He spoke through a rust-blotted section of wrappings which crisscrossed over his mouth—the blood stain of whoever's young penis he'd last bitten off from before his own limbs had fully developed. I feared that

------

The half of her body which he now manipulates forces her other into self-rape.

my neck would be bitten by him. With his other hand touching my lips, he forewarned:

Girl, you shouldn't ascend, for you'll find Christ has returned with a halberd but no longer has love for His people nor any reverence for my seven annelid gods. His art shineth not from His heart but from the line that He threads through the center of all that exists to the right or the left of antonymity. The halberd that He swings around is forged for cutting down all absolutes and carving through opposition and its impeccable opposite. Grafting these at their wounds, He intends to create an unconscionable monster of being, a being both neither and each. I can take you up there, but to lighten my load I must cut you in half. My worms will sustain you and keep you alive. When you see my lord, Yaldabaoth, clasp tightly the item I gift you and pledge the Eunuchs' Prayer for Divine Alliance verbatim—

Before I could pull myself free from his clutches, he unknotted his sharp shoot of stibnite—shoving its length from behind me into my thigh gap and thrusting it upwards in one cleaving motion past the crown of my head, through my midsagittal plane. He unknotted his worms from his wrappings and inserted them into the right half of my body before I could lose consciousness. The left

---

His own body has remained dormant for too many hours in the absence of his consciousness. He develops a small pressure ulcer upon the skin covering his tailbone. His divine spark is still tethered to it, even while venturing elsewhere.

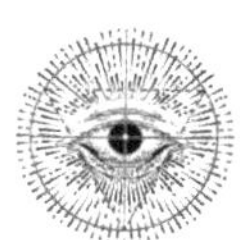

side was dead to me now, bleeding out on the ground. He whispered his prayer to me, and placed a pebble-sized nephrolith, inscribed with the numbers 3663, in the palm of my hand. He tied me to his back with an excess of wrappings before ascending the ladder with me. More time passed than I cared to acknowledge while clambering up there with him. I looked up and looked down. We were so far from both Heaven and Earth. I became dizzy with vertigo. I would reach middle age before rising into the clouds.

A halved passenger on his back as he climbed, I could do nothing but envision the firmament of the Pleroma; I was too out of reach from its otherworldly terrain. I hallucinated the battling shrieks of archangels and archons, and the shouting of women and men. Heaven was rendered into an abattoir of its own. Similarly to how the wyrms down below congregated over the dunes, the firmament was a glistening body of annelid worms. They rose and fell—a respiring pearlescent chest of translucence and slime, and the blood from the scene that my mind's eye currently fabricated flowed in small streams between them. And those Sophians who still were alive had been wrangled by these worms and held captive—either hog-

Without some intervening schism wedged between Subject R's mental and physical constitutions, each of these strained assets run the risk of being compromised. It is decided that no repositioning of his body or treatment should be administered during the lesion's progression. The four stages of pressure-wound progression are arranged to be shepherded under the auspices of the four-step process of intellectual disengagement.

tied, shrimptied, crabtied, or balltied by the tubular, threadlike and slime-coated binds that the worms contorted their bodies into. Higher up in the heavens, archangel-winged amphipteres bit and constricted their rivals, the sinew-winged worms. In turn, winged worms bound and devoured winged serpents. Feathers and sinews hailed down. People bewailed their own fate or that of their comrades, and there were some who prayed for death in the sheer terror of worms slithering in and out of a fallen crusader's empty eye sockets. Many beseeched the aid of the amphipteres, but still more imagined no amphipteres survived the last wave of the battle, and that they would be ever-forsaken along with their demoralized God.

Many Sophians had been left weirdly disfigured, silenced, and strangled by long, pearlescent ethereal worms. On vast bloodied stretches of firmament thousands of bodies were rotting in accelerated time-lapse. Sophians muddled and blended, their dried bodily fluids staining them the same rusted color. Blood hardened like plaster, pouring into their wounds, into the creases between them, over the worms enveloping their remains. Dried blood suspended the floor of the heavens in time, retaining a sculptural

---

Initially, his skin presents as reddened and does not blanch upon palpation. His pressure injury is silent; its future mouth is sealed. It cannot scream in agony; it is not yet an open wound. When this reddened skin breaks open, a raw and tender crater is exposed; the wound, which cries for the power above all power to have no mercy upon it, weeps to signify its unrelenting willingness for pain.

texture—subsuming the harrowing postures of agony, frailty, and surrender. The War on Heaven was lost and an absolute failure.

When we arrived, it was as I'd imagined it. Before me there was a semicircle of seven great pyramids made from the piled corpses of men—the tops of which were paved flat so the vertically-postured archons could uphold Heaven's regality. Yaldabaoth, the pale pink Godworm and demiurge, neither lion nor serpent as other Gnostic sects thought, opened its rounded, impeachable maw, which was rimmed by a thick, flowing mane of scarlet tentacles. Its six kindred archon-attendants resembled enormous, phosphorescent iterations of the dark-striped, broad-headed, and cannibalistic Hammerheadworm, the smooth, slender, and parasitic Roundworm, the exoskeletal, iridescent, and predatory Bobbittworm, the four-jawed, fleshy, and insatiable Bloodworm, the segmented, bristled, and toxic Fireworm, and the slime-spilling, lengthy, and lethal Ribbonworm, respectively.

All the Sophian battalions had been dismembered and left to be nibbled in piecemeal upon the muculent firmament, layered with lesser celestial worms. Priests and nuns

---

His sorrow spreads to layers deeper than his epidermis—some of which despair so wholly that the damages incurred are irreparable. A blister forms locally, a microcosm of the torments and struggles of his senses. Before his blister bursts, a quantum of his inner self is drowned within its pus. The lesion manages to reach the depths of adipose tissue. Yet there now emerges opportunity for his volition to become decoupled from its tenuous dependency on flesh.

MY BIDS ITSELF BE SEEN AS MY EGOIST
THEE DEMISE DOTH LINGER AS LONG

had been torn asunder, neither by the demi-gods nor their lessers but by some edged, mechanical means. There were immense altars and thrones that had been felled to their sides beside humongous, slaughtered maggots—decked and bejeweled in the garments of bishops—punctured by Sophian pikes, swords, and lances. I understood now why the Sophians chose to invade. This slime-lathered haven of so many detestable sights and malodorous scents was more so a hell than a haven for demons.

Before I could call for you, you roared a battle cry in a voice that was no longer mine. Beyond the pyramids of stacked corpses was a drum of enormous proportions—the head of it unsurprisingly made from the skins of large worms. When you struck at this instrument with your machete, it resounded with a noise I'm sure all would hear down below as they vomited and quaked from its doleful vibrations. In nauseating reply, lesser worms rose from the firmament bellowing like the most horrific trumpets that I'd ever heard. In no time at all, I reached the prescribed limits. My stomach churned, empty; your machete was carving through worms. You had not taken notice of me.

I was just like Sophia and you, just like Jesus returned with a halberd. Together, alone,

---

He allows for the temperaments encapsulated by the vacuoles within his fat stores to be starved. His body is reminded that the Church maligns all corporeal experience as adverse conditioning, especially those engineered for pleasure and discomfort. Subject R is encouraged to reject his form as former—a cadaverous impostor.

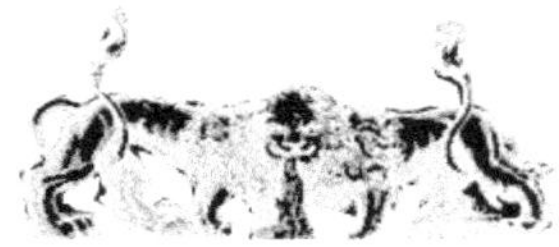

we formed the halves of a dyad—my silenced screams and your deafening silence, an absent presence for the absolute yielding to that which we still yearned. It was so bittersweet to see you again. I reserved feminine power to emanate substance, while you informed, through your masculine power, the substance emanated by me. Our sibling bondage would sublimate both estrangement and incest if we could be cleaved through ataxia and maintain continuity through revelation, in order to make indistinct where I was to end and where you were to begin—a circular roundworm, or round wyrm, with neither head nor tail.

A horde of worm worshipers wrapped in full body bandagings rose from the myriad ladders. I was released from the back of the eunuch who'd brought me this far, so that I could be laid before Yaldabaoth and so that the eunuch could rally with his fellow horde. You'd autopsy him and all his fellow martyrs whom you'd have the pleasure to murder. The archons observed from their pyramid tops, entertained. I looked upon them as if they were my emanations. The firmament parted before me—gesturing with an abominable invitation, so revolting that I couldn't help but oblige if only to get your attention. Yaldabaoth challenged our unspoken covenant with a shriek. It was the sort that could paralyze minds, but it held no such influence

---

Infection consumes him; the flesh he once had vanishes; a new skin, blackish-gangrenous, fills in and spreads across—a dark and rancid veil. Finally, his raw tissues are denuded to the bone; he's become susceptible to osteomyelitis and sepsis of the blood.

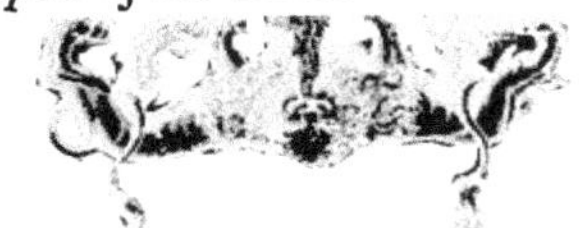

over me. Deliberate and lucid, I remained on my back, facing the demiurge—rendered so wretched from want that it must have emanated from me, and, so, therefore, it should return to the fount whence it came. My half-womb yawned open. I pressed the pebble-sized nephrolith, inscribed with the number, 3663, into the right of my spliced, spasming clitoris and then half-recited the Eunuchs' Prayer for Divine Alliance:

Hail, Yaldabaoth, stout tentacle worm, natural source of fire. And hail, gray water and splinter-leafed stibnite, and those who gather up wolf's bane and hawthorn from the fields of mechanical flowers, and who cause gentle foam to gush forth from pure mouths. Thelepus, the tentacle-maned polychaete, who once emanated from Sophia, O self-engendered one, because you are the demiurge of the Pleroma, two-syllabled as Saklas, two-fold as begetter and begotten, and are the first-appearing emanation, inhabit me, I pray: stay allied, lord, and listen to me, through my charm which produces direct vision which I have too today, and from mystic symbols hear what I declare as I say—

Perhaps if I'd finished the Eunuchs' Prayer, I could have asked Yaldabaoth for a miracle cure for our parents, but the demiurge wasn't long for the world. My dilated half sex,

---

He is wholly decoupled from his prior abode. Freed from its bodily subjection, he now resides exclusively within Subject L's right brain—wherein his consciousness has been projected. He is as she is—a unionized half-thing. Theirs are distinct and moietal intellects, each controlling one hemisphere of her body.

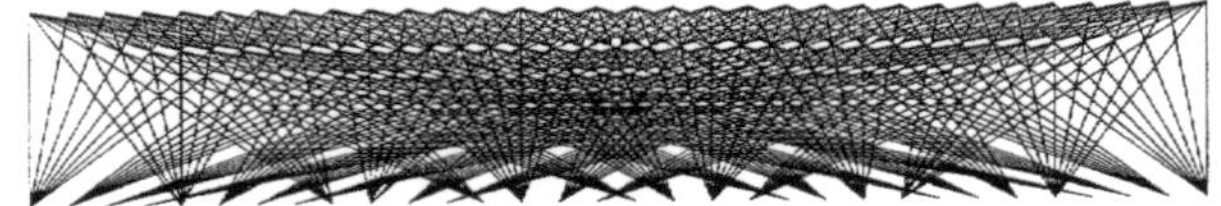

one venereal side of a Hellmouth, softened
its glistening labia. Yaldabaoth lowered its
mane, prehensile tendrils of scarlet. And the
eunuch's worms that sealed off my midsagittal gash slid their heads out and curled in like
fingers to signal 'come-hither'. The other
archons, who'd witnessed, recoiled at this.
Meanwhile, you'd been dispatching of their
worshipers—making slight work of them all,
slaying each with the sheer ataraxia of a mild
night's breeze. As for the archons, the arch-
worms, you had a way of staring them down
that could shrink them into diminutive size.
Thus, with your eyes, you belittled the Hammerheadworm until it reduced to the size of
a hammer; thus you belittled the Fireworm
until it reduced to the size of a cookflame;
thus you belittled the Roundworm until it
reduced to the size of a bootlace; thus you
belittled the Bloodworm until it reduced to
the size of a blood vial; thus you belittled
the Bobbittworm until it reduced to the size
of a bobbitted prick; thus you belittled the
Ribbonworm to the size of an arm's length
of ribbon—mincing them up with your blood
stained machete. Then, with blue-eyed fury,
you followed behind Yaldabaoth towards
me, shrinking that Godworm down to the

---

*Subject L fears Subject R's presence. She admits to no
longer feeling comfortable in her own skin. She threatens
to take her own life if he doesn't leave. The study could
have been halted indefinitely if not for the implementa-
tion of a divisive activity: Subject R is reintroduced to
the severed piece of his late wife's left sternum, while
Subject L is given the jar of 3,663 nephroliths—previously removed from her sender's late wife's right kidney.
These will serve as creative prompts for a forthcoming
assignment.*

size of an inchworm. Creeping up on it, pressing the might of your bare foot upon it, you smeared its fated existence across the firmament with the pitiless ball of your heel. You came to me next, unperturbed by my nudity and unsurprised by my presence. And the worms of the firmament bound my extremities. I was commanding them now to do so from your mouth—that voice of mine which remained localized to your left ear whispering, influencing, and convincing that physical side of you to tighten your grip on your bloodstained machete. Informed only by me, you had cleaved me to then cleave unto me and nothing else ever again. Raising the machete, with one clean overhand swipe, you turned its desiring blade on yourself—slicing down, from your crown to your groin, along the midsagittal plane. Your body split into two even hemispheres—your left side still trembling with life and the halo of consciousness. And I desired then to be wholed by the half of yourself which you'd cleaved from your other—that it would fall pristine and turn with precision as it fell to cleave to the half which remained of myself. Together we would pass through the subsequent stages—from this, our Separation, into Conjunction, from that Conjunction into Putrefaction, from that Putrefaction into Distillation, from that Distilla-

---

To gain better insight into their simultaneous independence, each subject is tasked with composing separate elements for an original story. Arbitrarily based on the oral traditions of the Church, Subject R drafts an elaborate backdrop and narrative with a keyboard, while Subject L develops the characters and the themes using a speech-to-text program.

tion into Coagulation. In the cleft of your self-made bisection, I hoped to contribute one half of myself to the process by which, with equal consent and refusal, our Magnum Opus could thus be transfigured.

In Sunday School we'd often slice butterflies lengthwise, mismatching and misappropriating their gender-coded halves to synthesize the divine through representation. Their diminutive scales would rub off on our fingers; we'd lap them up with our tongues. They tasted like cranberry seeds and worked into our brains like quick-release apothecarial acid. We'd lie on our backs with everyone else and hallucinate hovering signs of alembic, creative, hermetic, perfection-simulating transcendence—the Mother Superior, our Sunday School peers, and ourselves, melting and melding into the infinite, formless, timeless, and boundless Great Work. As close as we'd once come, we were so very far from it now. My half-tongue hung out between the occluded right arch of my teeth—I would have done unconscionable deeds for another brief taste of those scales. Through that most artful way, which neither ended in death or in coitus, we might have been struck with a timely epiphany that could assist us in consummating some semblance of an alchemical wedding, our unrequited syzygy—that raw forbidden intimacy for which we'd so long craved. But in this

----

After these elements are compiled into the tale which appears in the body text featured above, their work is confiscated, reviewed, then sent out to a research laboratory, unaffiliated with the Church.

wretched state, as we were, we couldn't go on as ourselves, nor could we fully let go.

We were cripples who'd collapsed just as we'd stepped within the inert and gravitational center of an interminable crossroads. We lay beside one another, stiffer than tombs but unable to fully repose. Coils of wyrms knotted in coils of worms fell from the sky of all skies as scale-and-slime garlands around us. And the worms which the Eunuch had packed in my wound reached out to grab hold of you but couldn't quite manage to bind us. Present tense was erased as it passed. All time and age remained incomplete. The future disjoined at the now and blacked out in its nearlies and almosts. We were left with whatever memories we could retain from the time of our severances, dating backwards.

Memories drained nearly as briskly as they flooded in. All that I thought of was now. At this juncture there stood a chance I'd forget and revert to retelling my tale and rephrasing all that I'd said to the very last line. I sensed the definitive certainty of this uncertainty. I could not foretell, nor could I concern myself with, what, if anything, would come next. And yet this was surely one half of the whole of the

Although this exercise proves that bifold embodiment can be achieved, the continued disputes over zones of autonomy between subjects contraindicate its utility. Moreover, the inevitable rejection of cohabitation remains at the core of the trial's clinical gridlock, and, so, partially